You're About to Become a

Privileged Woman.

INTRODUCING
PAGES & PRIVILEGES™.

It's our way of thanking you for buying
our books at your favorite retail store.

GET ALL THIS FREE
WITH JUST ONE PROOF OF PURCHASE:

◆ **Hotel Discounts** up
to 60% at home and
abroad ◆ **Travel Service**
- Guaranteed lowest
published airfares
plus 5% cash back

$50 VALUE

on tickets ◆ **$25 Travel Voucher**
◆ **Sensuous Petite Parfumerie** collection

◆ **Insider Tips Letter**
with sneak previews
of upcoming books

You'll get a FREE personal card, too.
It's your passport to all these benefits– and to
even more great gifts & benefits to come!
There's no club to join. No purchase commitment. No obligation.

Enrollment Form

☐ **Yes!** I WANT TO BE A **Privileged Woman.**

Enclosed is one *PAGES & PRIVILEGES*™ Proof of Purchase from any Harlequin or Silhouette book currently for sale in stores (Proofs of Purchase are found on the back pages of books) and the store cash register receipt. Please enroll me in *PAGES & PRIVILEGES*™. Send my Welcome Kit and FREE Gifts -- and activate my FREE benefits -- immediately.

More great gifts and benefits to come like these luxurious Truly Lace and L'Effleur gift baskets.

NAME (please print)
_____

ADDRESS _____ APT. NO _____

CITY _____ STATE _____ ZIP/POSTAL CODE _____

📖 **PROOF OF PURCHASE**
Pages & Privileges™
SAMPLE ONLY

NO CLUB!
NO COMMITMENT!
Just one purchase brings you great **Free Gifts** *and* **Benefits!**
(More details in back of this book.)

Please allow 6-8 weeks for delivery. Quantities are limited. We reserve the right to substitute items. Enroll before October 31, 1995 and receive one full year of benefits.

Name of store where this book was purchased_____

Date of purchase_____

Type of store:

☐ Bookstore ☐ Supermarket ☐ Drugstore
☐ Dept. or discount store (e.g. K-Mart or Walmart)
☐ Other (specify)_____

Which Harlequin or Silhouette series do you usually read?

Complete and mail with one Proof of Purchase and store receipt to:

U.S.: *PAGES & PRIVILEGES*™, P.O. Box 1960, Danbury, CT 06813-1960

Canada: *PAGES & PRIVILEGES*™, 49-6A The Donway West, P.O. 813, North York, ON M3C 2E8

PRINTED IN U.S.A

▶ DETACH HERE AND MAIL TODAY! ▶

"Oh. A baby."

Meg held the child gingerly a few inches in front of her, as if it were some form of off-planet life.

"Yes, a girl-type baby. You're familiar with the design?"

"Not so's you'd notice," Meg announced. "I happen to be a bachelor."

"Bachelorette," Jeb quoted from his extensive vocabulary.

"So you could put something on the kid and we'll go ahead with the interview."

"I've never...er...dressed a female. I mean of this size and age, you understand."

"From what I hear," Meg retorted, "you've dressed or undressed a whole bunch of women in your time."

She made an effort to hand the child back to him. He moved out of range.

"You're about to tell me, Mr. Lacey, that you've never diapered a baby?"

Dear Reader,

Urbanna is a lovely, real town. The Oyster Festival is well past its thirty-fifth year. The Wormelys were my ancestors, now long dead. And everything else is pure fiction!

Emma

Books by Emma Goldrick

Don't miss any of our special offers. Write to us at the following address for information on our newest releases.

Harlequin Reader Service
U.S.: 3010 Walden Ave., P.O. Box 1325, Buffalo, NY 14269
Canadian: P.O. Box 609, Fort Erie, Ont. L2A 5X3

THE BABY CAPER
Emma Goldrick

Harlequin Books

TORONTO • NEW YORK • LONDON
AMSTERDAM • PARIS • SYDNEY • HAMBURG
STOCKHOLM • ATHENS • TOKYO • MILAN
MADRID • WARSAW • BUDAPEST • AUCKLAND

To our eldest son, Michael, who labors at length, keeping
our word processors working

ISBN 0-373-03375-3

THE BABY CAPER

First North American Publication 1995.

Copyright © 1995 by Emma Goldrick.

Printed in U.S.A.

CHAPTER ONE

JEB LACEY lived in the old house in Urbanna because his mother preferred Paris, and his sister Gwen wouldn't touch the Rappahannock River and Southside Virginia with a ten-foot pole. The house was brick and stone and wood, mostly from after the fire of 1852. The windows didn't fit their frames, and rattled like ghost-walkers on a windy night. The two huge chimneys fed six open fireplaces—whenever they had been swept, which didn't happen very often. There were occasional leaks in the roof, and the driveway was a mass of mud in the springtime, but no matter.

So Jeb, who made a good living by writing—anything that any editor might buy on any subject—would spend three months at his word processor, then take the next three months off to go fishing. He kept a dog for companionship, an ancient collie who might have been older than the house. The dog responded equally well to 'Hey you' or 'Rex', when he responded at all. The dog was big and handsome. Jeb Lacey was merely big. Six feet two, thin, with light brown hair and brown eyes, a matching set of pearly teeth, and a pair of ears that were slightly bigger than necessary. Not Mr Spock size, but big enough to be noticeable. Oh, and a cheerful smile that, when flashing, caught any woman from six to sixty. All in all, Jeb Lacey was very happy with life.

And then, on a cool autumn night in September, Rex stirred along about ten o'clock at night and barked like a fool puppy, and the doorbell rang.

5

"Good Gawd, who is it?" Jeb muttered from the study. It was one of his working months, and his hero had just murdered the Crown Prince of Moldavia. The doorbell rang again. Rex actually made the effort to get up off his pile rug next to the word processor and ambled out to the door.

"Keep quiet," Jeb commanded. "They'll think nobody's home and go away." But a splash of wind rattled the windows, the doorbell rang again, and Rex sat down with his nose at the letter slot and whined. Jeb gave up.

"All right, all right," he yelled. "I'm coming!" His slippers were hidden somewhere or another. He barked his toe on the frame of the computer, said something nasty in four languages, and weaved his way out to the hall, using two hands to pull the sticky door open.

"Well, it's about time," his sister Gwen grumbled. "Here. Hold this."

It was too small to be a suitcase, and he hadn't seen Gwen in two years or more—hadn't wanted to, for a fact—and his mind was just not with it. "What is it?" he asked.

"Don't drop it," his sister grouched at him. "It's a baby."

She forced her way by him, stomping on his bare toe as she went. Rex stayed by the door. Jeb followed his sister into the living room, his eyes watering from his aching toe. It struck him suddenly how much he cared for sister Gwen. The baby cried.

"I need a place to put up," his sister said. "I suppose Mother is still in Paris?"

"Yes, indeed," Jeb said sarcastically. "Want me to get you a plane ticket to France? We have a dandy travel bureau up on State Route 227."

"Don't push," his sister groaned as she fell into a cushioned chair. "We just got here."

"I *did* notice," Jeb muttered. "Lovely child. He looks like——"

"*She*," Gwen snapped. "Got anything to eat in this mausoleum?"

"I—not much. I could send out for some pizza. Does the kid eat Italian food?"

"How can you write so many books and be so stupid?" Gwen asked disgustedly. "The kid's only eight months old. You don't know a thing, do you?"

"I guess not," he confessed. "I didn't even know you were married."

"I'm not," Gwen retorted.

"Oh." And a pause. "You'd like it in Paris. I could fix you up easily."

"Hate kids, don't you, little brother?"

"I don't hate them," he replied. "Who hates kids? I just don't understand them. Especially girl kids."

"So find us a place to bed down," his sister said as she stood up and stretched. "And get my suitcase. It has all the kid's clothes in it. It's out on the porch."

And that, Jeb knew, was the end of the Moldavian murder. So he turned off the switches on the computer, found a bedroom down the hall from his own on the second floor, and struggled with sheets and blankets and pillows. And milk. His sister had brought a quart of fresh cow juice, and she quickly showed Jeb had to prepare it before *she* went to bed.

Jeb sat for a while in the rocking chair, and fed the child. The baby *was* cute. She dozed off in her uncle's arms, bubbling little milk bubbles. He burped her according to instructions, then tucked her away among a pile of pillows on the floor, and sneaked out to his own room, three doors down. His sister snored, he remembered.

It was eight o'clock before Jeb awoke; the baby was crying, and Gwen might just as well have been dead for all the attention she paid. So although he cared not a wink for his sister, nor knew anything at all about babies, Jeb stumbled out of bed, and went down the hall and peered into the other bedroom.

The child had managed to roll over on her stomach, and had crawled halfway up the pillow-barrier he had erected the previous night. When she saw her uncle Jeb she rolled over on her side and gave him a big smile, and then started to cry again.

"Gwen," he muttered. His sister did not answer.

"For Gawd's sake, Gwen, wake up before your kid has a screaming fit." He reached over and shook the bundle of blankets. Gwen always slept that way, her body curled up, her head tucked under the blankets. But he was not the dumbest member of the Lacey family. When he shook the blankets for the second time it became apparent that Gwen was not under them, or in the room, or—as he discovered ten minutes later—in the house.

He checked his watch. It would be around lunchtime in Paris. He picked up the little girl and jiggled her over his shoulder as he dialed his mother's overseas number. She was just getting up.

"Gwen?" she repeated after him. "I haven't seen Gwen since a year ago. Why would she come here?"

"I don't know," Jeb said. "She was here last night, asking for you. Her and the baby."

"Her and the what?"

"Baby. B.A.B.Y. Now this morning Gwen's gone and the baby is still here. What do I know about taking care of a baby? Maybe I could hire someone to bring the kid over to you?''

"Don't you dare," his mother snapped. "Money yes, babies no. I had enough of raising babies with you two. And you didn't send me a check this month!"

"And I'm not going to." Jeb, frustrated, told the truth for once. "Not until I get rid of this kid. How do you figure Gwen leaving her child on my doorstep?"

"Why not?" his mother said. "Mothers don't necessarily have to love their children. Besides, you don't have anything much else to do except run that stupid computer machine. Why don't you write a bestseller for a change, instead of all those odds and ends?"

"Odds and ends that keep you fed and happy in Paris," he snapped, and then pulled the telephone away from his ear as his mother slammed the receiver down. He could have sworn she was laughing at him, and it hardly seemed fair at all. But then his mother and his sister had been living off his income for the past ten years.

He had left the baby upstairs on the floor, and now suddenly he noticed that the child was no longer crying. "Holy——" he muttered, and dashed for the stairs. The baby—didn't babies have names?—was squirming around the middle of the floor while Rex washed her face for her with his big rough tongue. Both of them seemed happy with the world.

Jeb leaned over and picked the child up. Soaking wet, she was. Dripping. Even an uncle knew that couldn't be right. The suitcase that Gwen had ordered to be brought into the house was now sitting, open, in a corner of the room. He grabbed a diaper off the top of the pile, added a dry undershirt and socks, wrapped the child in a towel, and took the whole mix downstairs. Rex tagged along behind.

The house didn't live on fireplaces. He pushed the central-heating thermostat up to seventy-five degrees Fahrenheit. There was a big metal sink in the kitchen. He stripped the child, filled the sink with lukewarm water, and sat the little girl down in it. She acted surprised, but courageous. She splashed a time or two to get the range, and then raised a fountain which bathed him more than it did her.

"Damn," he said. "Why me, God?"

His punishment began immediately. His back-door alarm went off, sending a shrill whistle throughout the house. The telephone rang. The doorbell rang. His radio alarm clock turned on and flooded the house with rock music. And the baby cried.

Jeb started for the door. The baby fell over and gurgled. He came back, wiped her off with a dry towel, and used another to wrap her up. The doorbell rang. He started for the door again. "I'm coming, I'm coming," he yelled as the thick oak door stuck. "I'm coming." He put the child down on the rug in front of the door and used two hands to force it open.

"Mr Lacey?" He picked the child up again, and double-wrapped the towel to protect against the chill.

"The only one in town," he commented. "But I don't buy at the door."

"At your office?" she asked.

He had the normal number of male genes. And she looked like a very great deal of woman. Five feet ten, perhaps, with honey-gold hair tied back into a ponytail, a figure that would give Venus conniption fits, deep green eyes, parchment-clear skin with a dash of color on each cheek. Just the sort of woman he didn't want to bother with—at this particular moment.

"I don't have an office," he said. "Who might you be?"

"Meg Hubbard," she said. "From the *Virginia Lady*. I have an appointment."

"Do you really?" He passed the baby over to her. "Come in."

She bustled through the door and he closed it behind her. "Oh. A baby," she said, staring. She held the child gingerly a few inches in front of her, as if it were some form of off-planet life.

"Yes, a girl-type baby. You're familiar with the design?"

"Not so's you'd notice," Meg announced. "I happen to be a bachelor."

"Bachelorette," he quoted from his extensive vocabulary. "Maiden."

She held up a one-handed stop sign. "So you could put something on the kid and we'll go ahead with the interview. I don't have a great deal of time."

"Me neither." He shrugged. "In fact I've never—er—dressed a female. I mean of this size and age, you understand."

"From what I hear," Meg retorted, "you've dressed or undressed a whole bunch of women in your time. Shall we begin?"

She made an effort to hand the child back to him. He moved out of range. "You might perhaps put a diaper on the babe?"

"I tend to believe you could do it better," she said stiffly.

"I don't see why you'd say that," he returned. "She happens to be a female—as do you."

''You're about to tell me, Mr Lacey, that you've never diapered a baby?''

''Not a girl baby.''

Meg sighed. Her editor had warned her about this interview. And about Jeb Lacey, for that matter. But not this. She held the baby up in front of her. Cute kid, no doubt. If you liked kids, that was.

''The one thing I *do* know,'' he cautioned, ''is that if you don't cover her—bottom—she may very well—er——''

''Yes.'' There was a long mahogany table in the study, covered with miscellaneous stacks of paper. She brushed one of the stacks off onto the floor and stretched the baby out. Out of the corner of her eye she could see that he was watching her like a hawk.

''You needn't be surprised,'' she said as her fingers fumbled with the diaper. ''I did this once fifteen years ago for my niece Sara.''

''Nice name,'' he mumbled, ''but you just threw Svetlana, the Princess of Moldavia, on the floor, and I have a twenty-day deadline on her.''

''I wish I knew what you were talking about,'' she returned. ''Where's the pin?''

''Pin?''

''Yes. Pin. To fasten the diaper. The kid can't hold the thing up with two hands.''

''Smart reporters seldom get good interviews,'' he said coldly.

Meg Hubbard flushed. The interview was important to her. Her editor had said so, her publisher had said so, and Mrs Macomber, who owned the whole shebang, had made certain threatening statements. The Urbanna Oyster Festival was not until November, and if Meg didn't get another assignment before then it would lead to hungry times.

"Observe," she said. "You put the diaper under here, and around there, and you—if you had one—pin the whole thing together. Now you try it."

"Not me," he objected. "How about a paper clip? Or a paper staple?"

"I don't see what's bothering you," Meg said. "She's only a little girl."

"I *did* notice."

"And, if you follow scripture, was created after Adam."

"And—what's your point?"

"Being the second model, women turned out considerably better than men. God, when *She* did this second work, you'll note, got all the plumbing inside."

"Here's the pin," he said, with a disgusted snort.

"What do you call the child?" she asked as she finished the job.

"I don't know. How about Rex?"

"You're the father of a child and you don't even know what her name is?"

"I'm *not* the father of the child, and no, I don't know what her name is. Nor do I know any reasonable way to find out. My sister dumped her on me last night."

"Well, Rex is a dog's name." The dog, hearing his name taken in vain, got up off his rug and came wagging his way across the room. The baby made hungry noises. Rex did the same.

"Well, we'll call her Maria," Meg said. "Now, what's for breakfast?"

"I don't know. I usually go up the street to the restaurant."

"You can't haul a child this age out to a restaurant."

"I don't know why not—it's a good restaurant!"

"Men!"

"Look, I've got a ton of work to do. It you're not happy with—er—Maria, then go do something about it. But leave me alone. I've a big family to support."

"Money," she responded, and held out one hand.

"I'm a reporter, not a banker. If you want me to buy food, put your money where your mouth is."

"Women," he muttered, and pored through his desk drawers. There was an assortment of currency, ranging from twenties to one hundreds. He stacked a few of them. A check book; he signed two blank checks. A credit card, unsigned. He passed everything over to Meg. "Stock the cupboards," he ordered, "but please leave me alone."

"And the baby?"

"Well, take her with you, of course. There's a suitcase upstairs in the green room filled with her clothes."

"I——" Meg hesitated. "I don't have forever to do this interview," she said.

"And I don't have forever to do this book," he returned, gesturing toward the papers on the floor. "These books."

"My grandmother told me about men like you," Meg said, sighing. "I didn't believe her."

"G'bye," he said. "Get a lot. I like Italian."

By midafternoon she was back, bursting through the big front door with a happy baby riding in a new child-tot. "C'mon," she yelled.

Jeb popped out of the study. "Now what?" he grumbled. "You're blowing my plot all to Hades."

"Plots I don't need," Meg responded. "Muscles I need."

He shook his head. Nothing had gone right since the baby appeared. Female baby. But he followed Meg out to the drive. She was using her own car, a 1992 van, loaded to the eyebrows. The library was across the street, in what was once a tobacco warehouse. The librarian came out onto the wide porch to watch and wave.

"All your neighbors keep a kindly eye on you?" Meg was there beside him, loading her arms with goodies.

"Keep a kindly eye? Nonsense," he replied as he dug into the food piles. "They all hate me. They expect me to donate copies of every new book I get published— for free, no less. I keep telling them I'm in the business of *selling* books, not giving them away."

"Watch out for the milk," she warned. "I could only get glass bottles." She said something else as well. Could it have been *Scrooge*? He wasn't sure, and so let it go by the board. But she was whistling as he brought in the next load. Whistling? Barking dogs and whistling girls will come to no good end, he recalled the old adage as saying. She paid it all no attention.

"I don't believe any of this," Jeb maintained on his fifth trip to the car. "All this we need?"

"All this *you* need. I can always go home to my gran's for dinner."

"Oh, no. Just a darn minute," he said. "You can't expect me to live through the night——"

"And you can't expect *me* to overnight with a male bachelor," she answered. "What do you think my grandmother would say about that, for goodness' sakes?"

"I wouldn't know. That's all the relative you have?"

"That's plenty. You *are* a bachelor? No wife in hiding, or something like that? A mistress?"

"Not anything like that," he said. "Now, what are you going to make us for supper?"

"*What?*"

In the end he showed pure genius about the supper. Canned beans and hot dogs, with ketchup and french fries. And for the baby a jar of mixed vegetables, which little Maria ate, but not with a lot of enthusiasm. When it was over Jeb managed to police up the little face, and found a smiling niece beneath it all.

He was startled. It wasn't something he expected. He leaned over and found a clean place on the end of her nose, which he kissed. Maria gurgled in delight.

"Now," Meg said, "you can start the dishes, and while you do that I'll ask you some questions for my article."

"That doesn't seem entirely fair," he protested. "I've got work to do in Moldavia."

"You've also got work to do in Urbanna," she said. Behind the kitchen door she found an old pinafore which looked as if it had been hanging there since the war between the states. She tossed it to him. He fumbled around with it and gritted his teeth.

While Meg collected dishes Jeb collected hot water and soap and a chair so that the baby could watch him. Just before the child fell off on her nose he snatched his one necktie from the study and used it to tie her in. At about that time Meg came out to join them.

"Telephone call," she announced.

"That's nice," Jeb said. "What did he want?"

"A she," Meg said. "Your sister."

"Dear Gawd," Jeb yelled as he stuck his finger under the hot instead of the cold-water faucet. "Watch the kid. I need to talk to that woman."

"Too late. She hung up."

"What? You let her——?"

"Just how do you suppose I could have kept her from hanging up?"

"Threats," he shouted at her. "Bribes." The baby started crying.

"Men! See what you've done?" Meg comforted the baby.

"So what did my sister want?" he asked softly.

"Two things. She wanted to know how the baby was, and she wanted to know when you would send her another check."

"And that's all?"

"And that's all. Oh, she did mention that the kid's name is Eleanor."

"Oh, Gawd, why me?" Jeb muttered.

"And she gave me the address for the check you're going to send her. She's in Atlanta, in Georgia."

"I know where Atlanta is," he muttered. "And you let her believe I'd send her a check?"

"Of course. She's your sister, isn't she?"

"Oh, sure. Rhett Butler will bring it to her the next time he sets the city afire. You know, like *Gone with the Wind*. Sister? You should have a sister like that, let me tell you."

"Well, I really wish I *had* a sister."

"Don't worry, I'll give you one," he threatened. "Just after I murder her. Why is it that I feel you're trying to get even with me for something?"

"Why, I can't imagine why," she said as she offered him a demure little smile. "Now, about my article. You were born in...?"

"Memphis, Tennessee," he said without thinking about it. "My father was Ralph Wormeley Lacey, and my mother was Leni Leoti."

"Wow," Meg said. "Ralph Wormeley? That's a famous name in these parts."

"So I've heard. My several-times grandfather was one of them. John of Cool Springs, they refer to him around here. Actually, in our family his son was known as Cold Water John. He was run out of the Shenandoah valley because he was a Tory Temperance lecturer."

"I don't believe that," Meg said. "You're making it all up. Who ever heard of a Moldavian princess named Svetlana?"

"Listen. It's my book. I can name the characters any which way I want."

"Yeah, but look out for the baby. She's falling asleep and is about to——"

Jeb caught the little tyke before she actually fell. Cute little thing, he told himself. I wonder who the father could be? He held the baby gently while Meg found a wet cloth and gave her a gentle hand bathe. And that's not bad, either, Jeb thought. I haven't seen honey-gold hair like that in a dog's age. Why don't I just talk her into my bed tonight? It's been almost forever since I had a good romp.

"Don't even think about it," Meg told him.

"What?"

"I'm a psychic," she told him. "I can read your mind."

"I don't believe in psychics," he announced. "You're a pretty good fiction writer yourself, aren't you?"

"So I'm going to take the baby upstairs," Meg said. "I bought her a portable crib. Look at the darling. Your sister must be some kind of beauty."

"Some kind is right," he agreed. "But lord knows *what* kind."

He watched hungrily as Meg went up the stairs. Long legs, well-shaped, altogether too sharp for her health— or mine. But out to get me. I can't let her get away with that. No way!

For another hour he worked in the study. It was true, he thought. There never was a Moldavian princess named Svetlana. That was a Slavic name. He turned to one of his favorite sources. When one needed a number of names, only a telephone book would do. A big telephone book.

He ruffled through the pages of the Middlesex County telephone system. And found a name that appealed to him. Hubbard. Where had he seen that name before? Margaret Hubbard? Of course. Meg. Long Meg, a favorite English name from the seventeenth century. And why couldn't he give her a hard time? Love *Little* Meg! His fingers diddled the dial before his conscience could catch up to him.

"Hello. Mrs Hubbard? I wanted to let you know that Meg is going to stay over at my house tonight. Yes, it involves her work. I'm Jeb Lacey, ma'am, and——" He moved the instrument a few inches away from his tender ear. "But ma'am—you know she wouldn't. Well, if you're going to take *that* attitude I don't think I *will* give you my address." With which he put the telephone down on its stand. It sounded as if Mrs Hubbard might be having a stroke. Or was planning a lynching party.

With a very self-satisfied smile on his face Jeb went back to work.

Meg Hubbard came back downstairs within the hour. The baby was fast asleep, her face registering happy dreams. As for herself, Meg was still not certain. Oh, it was true that she barely held her job on the Southside

Press, and only a good interview with Jeb Lacey would do her career any good. Beyond that? Hardly anything. Maybe a slot behind a counter at Bristows, but she shuddered at that. The last time she had worked behind a counter had left her with a vile disposition and tired feet. Even her grandmother couldn't approve such a job.

And so that left Be Kind To Jeb Lacey Week? Well, not *that* much. He was a nice man—sometimes. He looked—acceptable—when he smiled. Which wasn't all that often. And besides, a lot of women in small towns learned to get along with homely men!

And so into the study. He looked up—and smiled.

"How about a cup of coffee?" she offered.

"Tea. I don't care for coffee," he said, and put his nose down to the grindstone again.

"Tea? I can make that." She started for the kitchen, but his movements held her. Those long fingers of his were gliding over the keyboard of his word processor like greyhounds running a short track. He hesitated and looked up. Meg fled the scene. It was bad enough to be caught staring, never mind collecting all the smart remarks he probably would make.

The teakettle was under the sink. It looked as if it had been rescued from the *Titanic*. Rather than try to polish it Meg located a small saucepan and set the water to boiling.

To the right above the sink there was a cup cupboard. Containing one cup, and not a very clean one. Meg shrugged helplessly. How could you be nice to a man who lived like this? Against the opposite wall was a dish washer. She walked over and lifted the lid. It was loaded with dishes, cups, saucers, utensils, everything. They even looked clean.

The tea bags were no trouble to find. She had just purchased them up at the Park Side supermarket. And so, loading a tray with tea, cookies and condiments, she started back to the study. He was still at it, but looked up as she came in the room.

"What's that I smell?" he asked.

Meg looked down at the tray. There was nothing unusual there. "Cookies, hot tea," she said as she brushed off a space on the table. "You wanted something else?"

"No, I guess not," he said. "I was getting a little hungry but—that's not important."

"Can I ask you a question?"

"Well, of course. That's what you're here for, isn't it?"

"Yes, well—how fast can you type when you're working?"

"It all depends," he said. "When I have a clear line on the plot I can do about one hundred fifteen words a minute."

Meg took a deep breath. At her best level she might possibly make seventy words a minute. On sunny days, so to speak, when the wind was right. Of course, she told herself, speed isn't everything. It's *what* you write that's important. And the little voice of her conscience said, Nonsense, Margaret Hubbard. You can't even keep up to the secretary in the office! Which left a bad taste in her mouth.

She sat back in her chair, her feet straight ahead, balancing on her heels, and tried a sip of tea. Not that tea was her favorite drink. I am, she reminded herself, just learning to get along with the boss! She took another sip of the tea and looked at him. He had stopped work.

"I don't know," he said, drawling out the words. "I thought at first that the Prince would be killed by the Black Hand."

"The Black Hand?"

"A secret society of assassins. But now I think he'll be killed by the paramour of the Grand Duchess Sophie. With poison." He rubbed his nose as if it itched madly. "No, that won't do. Poison's out. The last story I did about Moldavia used poison." He leaned back in his chair and clasped his hands behind his neck. "It's hard to keep things straight," he said, sighing.

"How many—murder stories have you done?"

"Oh, about twenty, I would guess."

"Twenty? I thought—my editor said you've written a phenomenal number of books."

"Oh. I see. I meant that I had written twenty stories about murder. And some sixty or so thrillers set in England. Then you have to include about fifty romances in the Regency period, and perhaps sixty more modern romances. It's just too hard to keep track."

"Yes, I believe you," she said flatly. She had started calling herself a novelist when her first book was published. It had been followed by exactly none! She groaned. Her grandmother's favorite quotation was from the Bible. "Pride goeth before destruction, and an haughty spirit before a fall." And here it was.

"Something bothering you?" he asked.

"N-no," she stuttered. "I think I'll go out to the kitchen and——"

And the front doorbell rang.

"Good Gawd," Jeb said. "After ten o'clock of an evening. And who would be ringing at my bell?"

"All sorts of people," she answered. "Shall I——?"

"No. It's all a mistake," he commented. "There are exactly two buildings on this end of Virginia Street, and the other one is the library."

The bell rang again, more forcefully. It was one of those twist bells. The more energy the ringer applied, the louder the bell rang.

"Some kid," Jeb said. "They surely won't ring again." But they did.

Meg shrugged and headed for the front door.

"Damn," Jeb growled. "How in the world can I get this book finished?"

He flipped the off switch on the computer. There was no sense to wasting paper, not with prices what they were today. He heard the door open. Isn't that something? he asked himself. I have to put two hands on the knob to get it to open. This little lady can do it one-handed! Maybe I need more outside exercise.

He heard a murmur of voices in the outer hall. There was a light out there, but the bulb was burned out. Some day, he had said a dozen times or more. Some day I'll get it fixed.

Shadows crossed into the hallway. The kitchen light was on, as well as both the study lights. Meg Hubbard was leading the way. Behind her, hidden by her own size, was another woman.

"Mr Lacey," Meg said in a very subdued voice, "this is Annie Mae Hubbard—my grandmother."

Meg stepped aside. Jeb struggled to his feet. The woman confronting him was about five feet nothing, weighing in probably at one hundred pounds. Her face was remarkably smooth and clear, her hair white as snow, and she carried a black umbrella in her hand.

"Mr Lacey," she said in a deep strong alto, "just what are your intentions toward my granddaughter?"

CHAPTER TWO

MIDNIGHT, the witching hour. No traffic ran up or down the hill at Virginia Street. Windows, the seafood restaurant at the foot of the street, had long since closed. The docks along Urbanna Creek were quiet and dark. Across the creek, high on the hills of the other bank, ights still blinked in the great house called Rosegil. But the people who lived there were city folk, come down to Urbanna and the water for their summer vacation.

Jeb found himself out on the front porch with, strangely enough, his arm around Meg Hubbard. "Look at that," he said, pointing at the house across the bay. "My ancestors used to own that place. That and three thousand acres of land. Would you believe my first ancestor Ralph donated some three hundred acres on which Urbanna was founded? Now look!"

"What happened?" She nestled her head on his shoulder, just under his sturdy chin.

"What happened you wouldn't believe," he snorted. "Ralph Wormeley. His wife outlived him, married one of those weak-kneed politicians from down-state, and he took over everything, bag and baggage. But then, there were a lot of widows in those days who married and remarried. Women were an important commodity in colonial times. Especially women who had a proven track record with children."

"So then what happened?"

"With the Wormeley family? Well, after the Revolution they scattered. They were Tories, you know.

Loyal to Church and King. My great-uncle John moved out to the frontier—the Shenandoah valley. I told you about him. Eventually his descendants moved down into Tennessee and Memphis, where our branch of the Wormeleys grew up.

"Well, that was a long time ago, for a fact. I certainly wish I owned all those acres, and that fine house, but I'm not really jealous of them, whoever they are now. But the problem isn't *my* ancestors, it's yours. What do we do next?"

"What do *we* do next? It's your problem, not mine."

"Now wait a darn minute," he snapped. "It's your grandmother who's issuing all the ultimatums. Get married? Not on your ever loving life! That might have been the way of it in the nineteenth century, but not now."

"I feel pretty badly about the situation myself," Meg responded, moving away from him. "You are not, you know, the most handsome man in Virginia. In fact, I could throw a stone out into any part of Middlesex County and find a better-looking man than you are."

"Thank you very much," he said coldly. "Now that we have that settled, why don't you run along to Grandmother's house?"

"And leave you to finish *Murder in Moldavia*? You rotten man. You won't even give me the interview I need to keep my job!"

"Did I say that?"

"No, but you certainly implied that."

"A misunderstanding. You're welcome to stay as long as you want, ask as many questions as you need, and even help me with my murder. Just so long as you also help me with the baby. Do you know where Moldavia is?"

"No, I don't. Neither do you. It's all made up."

"Not Moldavia, my dear. It's my favorite murder scene. And, come to think of it, my favorite love scene as well." His hand came around her shoulders again. "Will you look at that fantastic moon?"

It was a foul blow. Meg Hubbard was a sucker for soft winds and moonlight. Especially a full new moon across the water. But this was not the man to tell that to. She bit on her lower lip and wished that she had her notebook in hand. She looked up at him; the moon was providing enough light to make him out. And he was grinning, that sort of lopsided grin that could easily set a girl's heart on fire.

"Meg," he said. "We never did get properly introduced. Margaret?"

"Not exactly. Margarete."

"You'd do great in Moldavia. Although I would probably have to change your name to—oh, Carlotta. Or maybe Griselda."

"Lord," she said, sighing. "Griselda?"

Her head was back on his shoulder, her lovely hair swathing him in pure gold. He gently moved her around to face him. Now what? she asked herself. It was not that she didn't know what came next in the script, but rather that there was a certain cosmic control over her that made her responses some thirty seconds too late with every little item. And so he kissed her without an objection.

It was a cool night, star-bright, moon-swept. But his lips were warm and commanding and moist, and it was many a day since she had been kissed with so much— élan. And the rascal knew it. He chuckled as he released her, and she debated whether she ought to slap his face or demand another kiss. Decisions were hard to come by, but she had help. Upstairs the baby fretted and began to cry. Almost automatically she moved out of his arms and started for the front door.

"Then you're not going home to your grandmother?"

"I—guess not," Meg answered. "Maybe the babe isn't all that important, but my article for the magazine is."

Together, hand in hand, they went in and climbed the stairs. And maybe the babe is all that important, she told herself. A man doesn't have to be all that handsome to make a good husband. Husband? Grandmother, get out of my head!

Rex was standing by the baby's door, his tail wagging vaguely. At his age the dog had little enough energy to get anything done in the dark of night. He led them into the room. Baby Eleanor had managed to get her head crammed into the far end of the crib, and her diaper was as wet as the Rappahannock River.

"Change her," Meg commanded.

"I'm not—sure," he said.

She brushed him aside and her busy fingers did the work required. "Why are men so helpless?" she asked. "Hold her while I get some of that formula I prepared earlier."

"My. You know all about that? Formulas and feeding and changing? Do you have any children of your own?"

"Don't be silly," Meg told him. "I read a booklet this afternoon at the drugstore."

"And that's all the time it took?"

"She's only a baby," Meg returned. "Now, change that blanket too. It's soaked as well."

By the time they had finished their whispered conference Eleanor was fast asleep again, her little lips going in and out, forming milk bubbles.

"I'll sleep in here in case she wakes up," Meg said, gently pushing Jeb toward the door.

"Why don't we share and share alike?" he offered. "The bed's big enough for two, and we could both get some rest."

"Oh, sure," she said sarcastically. "That's what my grandmother was talking about: sharing beds. But I, Mr Lacey, don't believe in recreational sex." With which she pushed him out the door. Rex followed him down the hall. He opened the door to his own room, then looked back toward the baby's room. That other door was firmly closed.

"Will you look at that?" he told his dog sadly. "I'm so dumb I didn't even know there was any *other* kind of sex available!"

Jeb Lacey had one very useful habit. He could climb into bed and drop off in seconds, and then he could wake up after four hours or so, totally refreshed. For a writer who made a big living from little contributions, it was an ideal habit.

On this particular day he awakened at the veriest hint of dawning, and was downstairs at his keyboard by four-fifteen. His fingers moved like magic. Lady Carlotta killed the Crown Prince, escaped to her winter dacha with her lover, was tracked down, and by six o'clock her vengeful father, with tears in his eyes, had shot them both dead. Dead, dead, dead. He loved that kind of an ending.

He ran the entire book through his spell-check procedure, noted the number of words on the front page, and slid the whole thing into a mailing envelope. Fifty-six hours from beginning to end—and everything that had happened in the house or the neighborhood was included: the baby, tears and all, Meg's grandmother, and a course of instruction on how to feed and diaper an infant. Jeb was that kind of a writer. He might not be *able* to diaper a little girl, but he sure as certain knew how to describe the affair.

He stood up gradually, sort of an unfolding process. Despite the battery-operated cushion behind his back, long exposure to the keyboard left him stiff. A squeaky greeting caused him the bring his head back. Meg Hubbard stood on the sixth stair down, baby Eleanor tucked under one arm.

'G'morning,'' Meg offered groggily. She had never been an early-wake-up person. Ten o'clock was a reasonable hour. Twelve-thirty was better.

Jeb looked her up and down. She was wearing an old robe of his mother's, who was somewhat shorter than Meg and considerably wider. Originally the robe had been yellow; over the years it had lost most of its color. Her golden hair came over her shoulders and down almost to her waist, and the baby was kicking and playing with it, full handfuls of guinea gold. With it all she gave the wonderful appearance of classic motherhood. Jeb's fingers itched to get it all down on paper, but Meg moved down the stairs and spoiled the pose.

"Good morning," he said. "Breakfast?"

"Looks as if you've been up all night," she commented as she stooped and put the baby down on the rug.

"Habit," he acknowledged. "*Murder in Moldavia* is finished." He held up the thick envelope. "I'll get it to the post office this morning."

"You mean you've really finished it?"

"Every word," he said, chuckling. "One hundred four thousand words. More or less. My counter isn't all that accurate. Eggs? Ham? Orange juice?"

Meg, who survived most days on toast and coffee, was about to refuse, and then had other thoughts. She knew men who could cook, but not many. Of those who could, none rated as pleasantly tempered at this early hour of the morning. It might be nice to—— "Yes," she said.

He gave her one of his quick one-sided grins. "All of the above?"

"As you say." She offered a neat little curtsy which was too much for the old robe. It slipped its tether, offering a briefly magnificent view of a great deal of woman, before her snatching hands could retrieve her modesty.

"Ah—yes," Jeb commented, and whirled around, heading for the kitchen. Unfortunately the baby, having passed her seventh month, had discovered a new world to explore. Sitting firmly on her little round posterior, she had discovered a way to hump herself along the floor. Not crawling, mind you, but *humping* at a considerable speed, with an occasional flop-over when she lost her balance. In any event she had advanced from the foot of the stairs until she was directly in front of Jeb's clumsy bare feet. And when he twisted and staggered and fell over the child, little Eleanor thought that a new game had been invented purely for her entertainment. She laughed and shook until tears fell.

"I don't really think it's funny," Jeb grumbled as he sat up, nursing his left knee. "I'm a war veteran, you know. Injured in service to my country."

Meg already had her notebook out, pencil poised. "Tell me more," she said, doing her best to hide her laughter. "What battle?"

"No battle," he snapped. "I was in the quartermaster corp. I sprained my knee moving hundred-pound sacks of flour. And if you print that I'll—I'll ruin your career!"

"Pretty hard to do," she returned firmly. "I don't have a career yet. Now, you were saying——"

"No, I *wasn't* saying," he muttered as he struggled to his feet and limped into the kitchen.

The baby followed along but got stuck on the threshold between the rooms. Meg snatched her up and carried her past the obstacle and over to the kitchen table. "You're not angry?"

"Me? Angry? Bruised but not angry. What does the kid eat?"

"Child. Eleanor. Not 'the kid'."

"Yeah, well——"

"You'll learn. Now tell me about your military experience."

"Why?"

"Any questions, any discussion, so long as I help with the baby. Remember that wild statement last night?"

"Boy," he muttered as he pulled out the frying pan and began to scrub it.

"Not *boy*, it's *girl*! You didn't notice?"

"I noticed," he grumbled. The pan was not exactly clean, but it was cleaner than it had been. He wiped it off with a paper towel, set it up over one of the gas burners, and cracked four eggs into it. And then he fumbled around in the refrigerator for slices of cooked ham.

"Well, I volunteered for the Gulf War. There weren't any draftees in service in that war. I ended up in the army. Armor, for a fact. But our division didn't have enough tanks, so I spent the first eight weeks with the quartermaster. And then the tanks came and the ground war started and we went off, and a pair of tanks from our own division made a small error and shot the hell out of us, and that was the end of my war. And my military service. End of discussion. Any question?"

"You were wounded?"

"Yes."

"Let me see where."

"Good lord, woman, have you no shame?"

"Oh. That kind of wound?"

"No, not that kind of wound." With one quick motion he stripped off his pajama top, just as the eggs began to smoke. "Oh, Gawd." He manned the spatula and tried to rescue the eggs. "Burned. I burned the damn eggs!"

There was silence from behind him, then a little whimper, and not from the baby. "I—I don't mind burned eggs," she said, choking on her words. "Not at all."

"I'm the one who was wounded and you're the one who's crying?"

"Oh, Mr Lacey. I didn't know. How could I know?" She threw herself at him and wrapped her arms around him, laying her soft cheek against the massive scar that was on his wounded back. "Oh, Jeb!"

"It looks worse than it is," he said gently as he tugged her around in front of him. "Now come on, girl, chin up. They gave me two aspirin tablets, a Purple Heart medal, and sent me home. Shortest war since the Israeli-Egyptian affair. I'm glad I could go, and happy I could come back. And I hope never to see the army again. Pull up a chair and—no, wait just a minute.''

He carefully grounded the spatula, looked over his shoulder at Eleanor, who was happily jabbering away with Rex, and then pulled Meg close against his naked chest.

She shuddered as her robe broke free again, cushioning the engorged tips of her breasts against him. And then he kissed her. For the second time, she thought as her mind went whirling away on the fingers of the storm wind that engulfed her. For the second time. Her bones seemed to turn to water—boiling water. Her breath was sucked out of her, leaving her panting under the pressure. And then he released her and loosened his grip.

She slumped slightly. A cool breeze separated them as he reached down, rearranged the fold of her robe, tightened the belt and re-tied it.

''There,'' he said mischievously, ''wasn't that nice? Eat your breakfast before it gets cold.''

''Yes,'' she gasped. ''Nice. Breakfast.''

And while she frantically fumbled with her fork Jeb Lacey sat down beside her, picked up the baby, and did his best to feed Eleanor from one of the baby-food jars. Eggs it was also, but flavored as badly as dog food. Nevertheless Eleanor ate with enthusiasm, some of it even getting into her mouth. And Jeb Lacey sat there, Meg Hubbard thought, with that stupidly wide grin on his face, as if he had just earned another Purple Heart. Maybe he had?

The post office opened at eight o'clock. Jeb arrived at nine. Everyone knew him. He was, they considered, one of the major supporters of the post office, a man who could be counted on, storm or strife, always loaded with a heavy manuscript, always prepared to buy a large load of stamps. This time he was also loaded with a baby carriage and a baby.

"Mr Lacey! What a pleasure to see you again. A new manuscript?"

"A new manuscript, Mr Ferber." A pause while the baby gurgled at all three customers in the office. "And how is every little thing among the postage stamps?"

"Always your little joke," the chief clerk said, laughing a dry little laugh. "Things go well. We have a couple of new stamp issues on hand and—I don't believe I've seen this little fellow before?"

"Girl," Jeb said firmly. "Newly come to live with us. My niece Eleanor."

"Cute," the clerk said. "A little girl? And not a hair on her head, hey? Oh, that's not true. Three hairs. Maybe four?"

"Some day," Jeb promised as he passed over his manuscript package. "Whole hog on this one, Mr Ferber. I want two-day service on this. It's bound to make my fortune."

"Overnight service wouldn't cost all that much more, Mr Lacey."

"All right, you talked me into it. Overnight service. My agent will be totally surprised. This will be the first time in ten years that I've beaten his deadline."

"Well! I'm glad to see that you're making some income, Mr Lacey." It was the acerbic tongue of a tiny old lady standing behind him, prodding him with her umbrella. Jeb wheeled around.

"Hey, lady," he complained. "Watch that umbrella."

"I'll watch it," she told him, not stopping her jabs. "And just where is my granddaughter?"

"Oh, Gawd," Jeb said.

"He won't help you. My granddaughter has been a praying member of the church for twenty-eight years, you monster, and now you've ruined her! God will never forgive you. Neither will I. Monster!"

"Don't be silly, Annie Mae. Your granddaughter isn't ruined. Hell, she isn't hardly even spoiled. I haven't laid a finger on her. As God is my witness, not a finger!"

"As Beelzebub is your witness, you mean. And don't call me Annie Mae. It's Mrs Hubbard to you, you philanderer!" With another jab from the umbrella. A sword stroke, meant to kill. And almost succeeding.

"Lady, don't *do* that. I'll call the cops if you don't cut that out. There's nothing wrong with your granddaughter. When I left she was busy working on her story for the magazine."

"So tell me when the wedding is," Grandmother Hubbard demanded.

"Wedding! Not on your life, lady. I'm not the marrying kind."

"Then we'll see about that," Mrs Hubbard yelled. "You've brought it all on your own head!"

"Lady," Mr Ferber said, "this is a post office. A federal office, mind you. Be polite."

"Be polite, hell," Mrs Hubbard yelled at him. "If you allow this man to buy stamps in your office I shall never ever buy another stamp here myself, and you can wager that all of the congregation of my church will feel the same way!"

Little Eleanor, wide awake in her brand-new carriage, finally concluded that the tone of voice was causing her dear man pain. She screwed up her little face, took two deep breaths, and told the world all about it.

"Now, now," Grandmother Hubbard said soothingly. She touched the tiny lips with her little finger—

and was seriously bitten by one of the three sharp little teeth that Eleanor already possessed. Grandmother said a nasty word three times. With some volume. A word appropriate to the farmyard, and not at all approved by the Church. Any church, that was. Grandmother stuck her finger in her own mouth to reduce the pain, and fled the premises.

"Well," Mr Ferber said, "as far as I'm concerned she can take her business over to Saluda."

"I didn't know they had a post office over at Saluda," Jeb said.

"And how about that?" Mr Ferber said, and winked.

Jeb Lacey made four more stops at various shops in downtown Urbanna before he took himself and his niece back down the hill at Virginia Street. The librarian, in the building across the street from his house, obviously on the watch, came out on the porch and waved to him. "Hello, Mr Lacey. How are you and your—baby this bright fine day?"

"Bright and fine, Mrs McGruder," he called. "Lovely day. Little Eleanor loved the walk. I think she'll make a fine citizen of Queen Anne's City when she grows up."

"Eleanor? Lovely name. An old family name?"

"I guess you could say that. There's one in the family, anyway."

"Mr Lacey, you *are* a wit!"

"You're half right, anyway," Jeb muttered under his breath as he crossed the street and went up the drive. Meg was waiting for him on the porch steps. She came down to the carriage and held out her hands toward Eleanor. The child responded with great glee, making noises that might possibly be interpreted as greetings. Meg picked her up and started back up the stairs.

"Well, she surely welcomes *you*," Jeb said morosely. "How do I get this carriage thing up on the porch?"

"Muscles," Meg called back over her shoulder. "Turn it around and pull it up one stair at a time, backwards. Bounce it."

"Yes, but——" Jeb called, but his two women had already gone into the house. Bounce it up, he told himself. Backwards. Women do it all the time. It's bound to be easy. There were six steps to the outside stairs. Fifteen minutes later, perspiration running down his neck, he managed to park the carriage on the porch and set the brake.

The two of them were in the kitchen. Meg was making little cooing noises; Eleanor was responding happily.

"Well, I mailed *Murder in Moldavia*," he announced, as if it were some great new accomplishment.

"How nice," Meg said with all the enthusiasm of a dead mouse. Eleanor said not a word. "Your sister called."

"Oh, lord." Jeb managed a word or two—in fact, repeating the word Annie Mae had used in the post office. It didn't sound any better in his kitchen than it had at the stamp window. "What did she want this time?"

"The same thing she wanted last time, she said. A check."

"You'd think money grew on trees down here," he snarled. "Where was she calling from?"

"Toronto, Canada. She said she was in a lot of trouble and had to blow the country."

"Well, Toronto isn't far enough," he commented. "Not if she's really in trouble. We have an extradition treaty with Canada, you know."

"No, I don't know. She's your sister?"

"And so I should send her a check? Hah!"

"She also said you'd be very, very sorry if you didn't send her a check. Very sorry."

"I'm already sorry," he grumbled. "What did she say about the baby?"

"Nothing. And then your mother called."

"Don't tell me. She wanted a check too."

"And that's not all," Meg said. "We talked about this and that. It seems she knew my mother. They went to school together up in Richmond."

"So I should give my mother a check because she went to school with *your* mother?"

"No, I don't think so. My mother died seventeen years ago!"

"Oh, lord, I *am* sorry, Meg."

"You needn't be. It was a long time ago. Do you know that's the first time you've ever called me by my name? I like that."

"I—is that so—Meg? Well, let's not get too taken with name-using. We have a business relationship, you and I. And my mother went to school with your mother?"

"Nonsense. My mother never went outside the boundaries of Middlesex County."

"I don't follow." Life could get to be very confusing, Jeb told himself, if she can make a simple statement and leave me wandering through the bullrushes. The woman's a beauty—and she knows it. Give her an inch and she'll run away with the whole place! Have a care, Jeb Lacey!

"Yes, you do. You're one smart cookie, Jeb Lacey, but why are you talking to yourself? Your lips are going ten miles an hour. No, my mother obviously never, ever went to school with your mother, which means that your mother lied to me. Is that a habit in the Lacey family?

Why, do you suppose, she would lie to me? Long-distance, too."

"If I were supposing, I would suppose that my mother figures that since I now have a woman in my house she must be of considerable importance to me. And therefore, whoever you are, my mother would like to get on your good side. Two things my mother can't stand are not having a lot of money and having to work for it. They call me the family cash cow."

"Bull, surely? And..." Meg paused and decided to change the subject. "Notice the nice new high chair."

"Nice," he said.

"A man brought it. I don't know who he was."

"I do."

"You ordered it?"

"It was right by the baby carriage. They were having some sort of baby sale. I mean, not a baby sale, but a furniture sale relating to babies."

"And you just bought them both?"

"And a new larger crib to go with it. It seemed like the thing to do."

"My goodness. You're a man of money today."

"Well, we all deserve it, don't we? *Murder in Moldavia...*"

"You're just so darn sure that it'll sell?"

"Positive."

"In that case I made you some tuna-fish sandwiches. I hope you like tuna fish?" Her question was accompanied by an anxious look. One thing Meg knew from her brief experience with men was that a girl could never be sure how they were going to respond. To tuna-fish sandwiches, for example.

"Love tuna fish," he said. It wasn't quite true, but what the hey?

Meg moved to the refrigerator and brought out a tray of sandwiches. "And a glass of milk?"

"Couldn't be better. Where did we get the milk?"

"I made an arrangement to have it delivered."

"Efficiency," he congratulated her. "We're really set up in business. How's your article going?"

She took a precautionary step away from him. "I found—your diary," she half whispered.

"Well, how about that? It's been lost for more than a year."

"And I used it to flesh out the early part of my article." She took another step backward. "And then I found your military file. One Purple Heart? Baloney. Four of them, and the Silver Star to boot!"

"Meg—I would rather you didn't write about that. I was never a hero. I knew a lot of heroes, but I was just a dogface—a plain ordinary soldier."

"I—don't believer that," she said, "but if you don't want me to use it I—it would make a great hook for my article."

"I suppose it would," he said, sighing. "Well, use whatever you want. Now, about those sandwiches."

So three heads dug into the variety of food, three heads drank milk, and when she was finished Eleanor managed to grab a spoon in both little hands and proceeded to play drummer-girl. Apple sauce flew like astronaut's rations, all over the kitchen.

"I can see," Jeb said, "that we'd better hire a cleaning woman for at least a couple of days a week. Could you see to that?"

"You can't?"

"Don't have the time. Have to get *The Devil Duke* on the computer. It's got a thirty-day deadline."

"*The Devil Duke*?"

"A historical romance, set in England in 1815. What we in the trade call a Regency."

"Lord, when do you stop?"

"Whenever I feel I need to." He grinned at her, leaned over, and touched her lips with a momentary kiss. "That's when I go fishing."

She stared at him for a moment, her chin resting on her hand. "Jeb, would you tell me something?"

"If I can."

She blushed and ducked her head beneath her mountain of golden hair. "When your mother——"

"Yes?"

"You said——" And then quickly, as if trying to get it out, "You said she must have thought that there was a girl living here and that you would have a—great deal of concern for her."

"Yes?"

"Would you?"

Jeb Lacey debated the subject for a moment. He had never thought about the idea in particular. Not in the manner of a you-me subject. Oh, there had been plenty of times when he had used it as a plot gimmick, and half a dozen times he had used it as the basis of a six-night stand, but for real? Think fast, Lacey; this woman deals only in reality, he told himself.

"Yes," he said, his tongue straining because it was dealing with the truth. "I would. I do."

CHAPTER THREE

THE deliveries started to arrive at about two o'clock in the afternoon. A seemingly endless line of trucks, big and small, pulled up to the old house on Virginia Street, and disgorged everything one could think of, from a huge new freezer to food with which to stock it. A new large baby crib, carried upstairs and assembled by the delivery men. A disposable diaper service, complete with instructions. A playpen, well padded, set up downstairs in the living room. A layette table and bath, six boxes of dog bones, what seemed like a ton of baby food, each item in its own little jar. And a box addressed to Meg.

"What in the world...?" she exclaimed as she gave up work on her own manuscript and came out to watch. Each item came accompanied by its own assemblers. Except for the box for Meg.

"I was going over to Grandmother's to pick up some clothes," she said as she balanced the box addressed to her, doubtful about opening it.

"That's what I forgot to tell you!" he exclaimed. "I ran into your grandmother this morning over at the post office."

"Oh, you didn't! What did she have to say?"

"I don't rightly remember. She was busy trying to stab me to death with her umbrella and I was busy trying to dodge." He made a little face. "She was better at her stabbing than I was about dodging. She made some remark about her church congregation praying for me, or against me, or something of the sort—I don't re-

42

member exactly and I *think* she threatened me with some sort of picketing. It's hard for me to remember exactly. Open the box, Meg.''

''I—I'm embarrassed. My grandmother was always a sweet lady.''

''I'm sure she still is. She just doesn't like me. It happens, you know. Open the box, Meg.''

Meg looked at him as if she couldn't believe the insinuation. A woman who didn't like Jeb? Almost impossible, right? Her hands wandered vaguely over the surface of the bright, glittery box, then seized on a seam and ripped. The box tumbled open. She set it down on the study table and pulled off a layer of thin packing paper.

''Oh,'' she said, startled. ''I've always wanted one of these. What is it?''

''You have to take it out of the box. It's something to wear on a cold winter morning.''

Meg shook her head, but plunged both hands into the box and pulled out a long golden robe, the match to her hair. Satin and silk, it was, with a set of over-large buttons and a large belt, guaranteed not to slip at the wrong time. ''Because of this morning?''

''Not exactly. Because I wanted to see you in something like that.''

Meg turned blush-red. ''I've never had a clothing gift from a man,'' she said. ''Are you sure it's proper?''

''If your grandmother doesn't see you in it I'm sure it'll be proper,'' he promised her. She blushed again. Blushed prettily. For a big woman, Jeb told himself, she's one cute little bundle. I could very easily—no, I couldn't. Marriage is too much to ask!

The clatter of delivery and assembly slowed down. Jeb signed a dozen or more slips, the last crew swept the floor and moved all the containers outside, and quiet descended. In fact it was so quiet that little Eleanor could be heard snoring away, and Rex could be heard dreaming. It must have been a successful dream because every now and again the big old dog would give out an excited whine, followed by a little yip.

"I have to—to get on with my article," Meg murmured as she sat down in front of his favorite computer. "I've finished the first section. It's a serial report, you know. It'll appear in the next four issues of the magazine. And, my editor tells me, they may summarize parts of it in the newspaper—the *Southside Sentinal*."

"If your grandmother sees it she'll probably break into the building and burn the place down."

"Don't be silly," Meg said. "My grandmother is eighty-two years old. She is usually a sweet old lady. What she has against you I just don't know. You're really a sweet man, you know."

Jeb gulped. He wasn't usually referred to as "a sweet man". Not even by his sister and mother, who were never ones to hold back on describing him. "But your grandmother has some wild friends?"

"I wouldn't say that either. Please don't pick on my grandmother. She's all the family I have left, Jeb."

"OK. I surrender. I'll try to avoid her in the future."

"And thank the Lord for that," Meg said. She fumbled around at the printer and collected a good double handful of printed matter. "So now I'm going to take this section up to the office, and then I'm going over to Grandma's to collect some clothing—and in the meantime you watch the baby. She's having a good nap, but she's bound to wake up sooner or later."

"Hey, she's only a baby," he boasted. "And I'm sure I can take care of her little needs. And in the meantime I'll knock off a chapter or two of *The Devil Duke*."

"Then I'll go along. Grandma will be at her garden club this afternoon.'

"Er—don't you think you ought to get dressed?" he suggested. "Downtown Urbanna is not much for women on the streets in their dressing gowns."

"Oops. I didn't——" Meg turned blush-red again. "Yes." She dashed for the stairs. Rex, stretched out on his rug in the corner, lifted a curious ear and then went back to sleep again. Jeb did his favorite imitation: Groucho Marx with his raised eyebrows and a leer.

When she came back downstairs Meg was dressed in the same outfit she had worn the day before, when she first came calling: a white sleeveless blouse, a conservatively cut blue skirt, and a pair of blue sandals. She peeked into the study. Jeb Lacey was already deep in the work of—what did he say? *The Devil Duke*? The man had more plot lines than Heinz had pickles! What an imagination! Eleanor was asleep on her stomach in her new playpen; Rex was also asleep, with his big muzzle crammed up against the bars of the playpen. Waving them all a kiss, Meg started for the front door.

It was a beautiful afternoon. High clouds scooted east, out toward the sea—clear white cumulus clouds, with never a threat of rain or storm. Meg stretched, up on her toes, to her farthest height. It had been a strange twenty-four hours, but in her leather briefcase she had the workings of a fine piece—the best writing she had ever done, and she was proud of the work. The baby was a little doll. She had always had an affection for babies, and to—acquire one practically painlessly was a joy. The dog was a gruff old farce; Jeb Lacey was...

She paused and took a deep breath. What was Jeb Lacey? Well, first of all, not as homely as first she had supposed. Not handsome by any means, but—nice. As her grandmother used to say, "A girl has to be good-looking; a man only needs to be employed!" And this he was. Totally employed!

The idea brought a giggle to her lips. A big girl, a big giggle. She shrugged, skipped down the six stairs to the ground, and wandered over to her car, where she came across the first impediment of the day. A man was leaning against the middle door of her van. An unknown, shady-looking man.

"G'day, little lady," he said. A deep voice, a firm face in need of a shave, a brown suit that could have used a press. And brown hair, which skipped a spot or two on the top of his head. He stood six feet up and down. In her heels she looked him straight in the eye. She looked him up and down. "Don't speak to strange men," her mother had always told her. But Meg Hubbard had found that half the fun in life came from speaking to strange men.

"G'day?" she queried. "You're Australian?"

"Not likely," he said, chuckling. "Pinkerton."

"I'm afraid I don't know where that is."

"What, not where." He reached into his pocket and pulled out a small gold badge. "Pinkerton Detective Agency."

"Oh, that! You're a—private eye?"

"That's about right. Mind if I ask you a question?"

"I don't mind—if you don't mind that I might not answer."

"Fair enough. I'm looking for a woman."

"We don't have a district like that," she answered
pertly. "Maybe if you tried over in Saluda?"

"No, no. I'm looking for a specific woman named
Gwen. Would she happen to live here in this house?"

"I doubt it," Meg said, suddenly overwhelmed by
caution. "Actually the only two females living in this
house at the moment are myself and the baby. My name's
Meg, the baby's name is Eleanor."

"And no other women—to your knowledge—have
ever come to the house?"

"Well, there's my grandmother—Annie Mae
Hubbard. She's come a time or two. What is it you want
with this Gwen something or other?"

"She's wanted in the State of Florida for
childnapping."

"Childnapping?"

"Yes. She kidnapped a baby and fled the jurisdiction.
Of Florida, that is."

"She must have had some urgent reason for that,"
Meg said slowly. "Kidnapped a baby? I wouldn't blame
her in the least. Her husband must be some sort of
gorilla."

"Not exactly her husband, either," he said. "And this
baby you have——"

"Is *my* child," Meg said firmly. "Now, if you would
kindly go away, Mr Pinkerton... In a moment or two
my husband will be putting the dog out, and Rex has
no liking at all for strangers."

"All right, lady." He straightened up, wiped his
smudged fingerprints from the side of her car, nodded
politely, and walked out to the street. But did not disappear. Meg watched him as he crossed the street to the
library and climbed the stairs.

"Up to no good," she muttered to herself. "When I get back from Grandmother's I'll have to tell Jeb all about it. Except for the part that Eleanor is *my* baby, and that Jeb Lacey is *my* husband. Or even that Rex would come out and *bite* him! How many lies have I come to tell since I moved into this house? And all for want of a story about Jeb Lacey. I hope the Lord would forgive me; I know Grandmother never would!"

With which she climbed into her car. And was promptly punished because the darned automobile wouldn't start. Not right away, that was. She ground the starter so many times that Jeb came to the front door. "Need some help?" he called.

Meg shook her head, stabbed at the starter again, and heard the refreshing noise of a running engine. "No, thanks," she called. Jeb waved and walked back into the house. Meg scanned the road in all directions. The private eye had disappeared. Probably milking the librarian for everything she knows, she thought. And Lord knows, she knows every bit of gossip in town!

Grandmother Hubbard lived in a small house on Kent Street, facing the Rappahannock River. When Meg drove up it looked like a Shriners' convention. Not only was Grandmother at the garden club meeting, but the meeting was at Grandmother's. And once she turned the motor off Meg was trapped. Gossip in Urbanna traveled faster than a jet airplane at thirty thousand feet.

She managed to fight her way out of the car, smiling in all directions as best she could—until her grandmother caught her arm and ushered her into the house. "Why do you have the collossal nerve to come back here?" her grandmother hissed. "A kept woman! Your grandfather would turn over in his grave."

Take the bull by the horns, Meg told herself. All eyes were on her; every club member with a hearing aid had it turned up to full volume. There were many more than one of those in the house.

She mustered up her loudest voice. "Working on an article for the *Virginia Lady*," she announced cheerfully. "Mr Jeb Lacey, you know." Fifty women were in the house; half a hundred knew Jeb Lacey by repute. "Jeb Lacey," she repeated. "Of the Wormeley family."

Another hiss of recognition. Hardly anyone knew that Lacey was from a branch of the Wormeley family: *everybody* knew that Ralph Wormeley was one of the founders of colonial Urbanna. The name echoed and re-echoed across the house. "Wormeley—Wormeley—Wormeley!"

"I'm doing the story of his life," Meg continued. Her grandmother winced; the remaining ladies applauded. "He's a war hero, you know."

"A war hero?" Even Grandmother softened. Her husband had won a good conduct medal in the Second World War. "Yes," said Meg, driving in the needle. "Four Purple Hearts, and..." a pause to let the suspense rise "...and a Silver Star!"

Letty Raeburn was chairperson of the VFW Women Auxiliary. "The Silver Star," she gasped. "Why, that's way up there next to——"

"Next to the Congressional Medal of Honor," Meg supplied. It wasn't something she knew offhand; it was something her editor had told her when she'd stopped by to let him have a read of her work so far.

"What an honor," Letty said. "And we never knew. Everybody in this town should be doing something to help him out."

"I do believe you're right," Meg said as she swept through the crowd and up the stairs. When she came back down with most of her worldly goods stuffed in a bag the tongues were still at it. Her grandmother met her at the foot of the stairs.

"I'm certain sure that it's not as bad as I thought, Meg," she said, "but surely you're not going back there?"

"I have to," Meg said loudly. "Not only do I have to finish the article, but then there's the baby——"

Another splash of conversation. "*What* baby?" Grandmother insisted. "Certainly not *your* baby?"

"No, not mine," Meg said. "Although she's such a sweet little thing that I'd love to adopt her!"

Grandmother's face crumbled. "Marriage," she whispered. Her words were drowned out by a round of applause from the audience.

"Of course," Letty Raeburn said. "No man knows enough to take care of a baby. Mr Lacey obviously needs a good woman to help him out. It's his baby?"

"His *sister's* baby," Meg said. "Gwen was unable to take care of the child. She's ill—Gwen is, that is—and very poor."

"Very poor". The words whispered their way around the room.

"But Mr Lacey, he *writes*, you know. He has more money than he knows what to do with! And he doesn't mind in the least spending it on the child. You should see the things he bought today."

"What? What?" The echo ran around the room again and again.

"But I have to go," Meg said sadly. "Four o'clock feeding, you know."

Everybody knew. Another round of applause chased her out the front door, her grandmother clinging to her arm. On the sidewalk, the pair of them alone, Meg looked down at her grandmother. "Well, Gran?"

"I might *possibly* have been wrong about him," her grandmother muttered. "But—marriage, Meg. Marriage."

"I'm sure it would be nice," Meg acknowledged. "You can lead a horse to water, but you can't make him drink!"

"Oh, my," Gran said, a tear forming in her eye. "Like that, is it? Well, don't go too far without the ring, love."

Meg leaned down—very far down—and kissed the lady on that little bald spot on the top of her head. "I'll try to be careful," she said. "But now I've got to run."

"God bless," her Gran said. "Another time I won't hit him with my umbrella. But——" she raised a warning finger "—I can't promise to respect him for what he's done. Now if you were his wife——"

"Yes, Gran," Meg interrupted, quoting another of those sayings that her grandmother had pounded in her ear over many a year. "If wishes were horses, beggars might ride." She gunned the engine and turned up Rappahannock Avenue toward the center of town.

Jeb had his head buried in the computer when Meg struggled into the house, pulling her bag behind her. Rex whoofed a single short greeting. Eleanor rolled over, looked around the unaccustomed playpen, and started to whimper.

"Well, I got two chapters done," Jeb said, rising to stretch. "Brought everything with you?"

"Almost," Meg said. She dropped the handles of her bag and went over to the playpen. "How's my little girl?'' she teased as she leaned over the child. The baby kicked her heels and grabbed for the cross that Meg wore around her neck. "Change time," Meg said, picking her up and carrying her over to the layette table. "It's a lot easier changing her with these paper diapers," she commented. "Have you tried it?"

"Me? I've been up to my ears with *The Devil Duke*. Your grandmother didn't burn you at the stake?"

"What kind of an idea is that?" Meg demanded. "She was very sweet. She sent you her—well, not exactly her love, but she did say she wouldn't stab you again with her umbrella. How about that?"

"I don't know how about that," he grumbled. "My ribs are still sore. But I've gotten even with her."

"You have?"

"You bet. She's turned out to be the villainess in *The Devil Duke*."

"Down deep in your heart, Jeb Lacey, you are a mean man!"

"So. You *did* notice. I've got work to do."

"I think you'd better just hang on for a minute," she told him. "I have to get the baby's bottle, and then I have something important to tell you. Something very important."

"OK, I can use a break. And I wouldn't want to miss anything coming from the Little Old Lady's Assault Society!"

"Oh, shut up," she said. "Would you like a cup of tea?"

She didn't wait for an answer. As far as she knew men *always* wanted a cup of tea, coffee, or alcohol. Which was strange, because she had yet to see Jeb tossing back a whiskey. Not yet, that was. But, if luck was on her side, she would see everything one of these days.

Meanwhile her busy hands snatched a prepared bottle of formula, heated it briefly in a little saucepan, made the tea, and offered the milk to the baby. Eleanor nuzzled the nipple for a moment, toying with it, and then settled down to do some serious gulping. She was at an age where she could hold the bottle for herself. Meg nestled her in one arm, managed the teapot with the other, and eventually went back into the study.

Jeb was still standing by the computer, stretching. "Getting old," he said as he reached for the pot and poured himself a cup. He drank his tea black and strong.

Meg lay the baby back in the playpen, poured herself a tot of tea, and pulled up a chair next to the computer.

"So, what's all that wonderful?" Jeb asked. "You went to see your editor?"

"And he loved the story," Meg said, grinning. "I think I ought to demand a raise."

"That's what you need an agent for," Jeb said. "You be the good guy while he bes the bad guy."

"Bes?"

"Bes. Don't ever let the language lead you, lady. So he loved the story. And then?"

"And then I drove over to Gran's house, and the garden club was meeting there. Lord, I haven't seen some of those women in a dog's age."

"Never mind the club; what about your grandmother?"

"She said—let me see now. She said that she would never hit you with her umbrella again!"

"Well, that's a step in the right direction," he said, chuckling. "I had ordered a bullet-proof belt, but I guess I don't need it, huh?"

"Well, now—she says that she won't assault you, but she's not exactly in love with you—because of you and me."

"I understand. The magic word with your grandmother is 'marriage', right?"

"Have no doubts," Meg said, wincing. "But if it's not peace, at least it's a truce."

"Not to be sneered at." He congratulated her as he reached over and kissed her gently on the tip of her nose. She was sitting in a wheeled chair. Puzzled, she shifted away from him an inch or two.

"What was that all about?" she whispered.

"Niceness," he said. "You made a great peace treaty. Besides, every woman deserves a kiss now and again."

Does she really? Meg asked herself. I never knew that. Listen, the voice of her conscience dictated, take all you can get. We all grow old!

"But that's not the part I wanted to tell you about," she said. "When I went out, there was this man."

"Oh?"

"Standing by my car. He said he was a private eye, and he had this gold badge and stuff like that."

"You *saw* the badge?"

"Yes, he showed it to me. A lovely gold thing that said something something Pinkerton."

"Ah. Pinkerton. I used them in a story last year. So what did this private eye want?"

"I'm not exactly sure. He said something about a woman named Gwen. He didn't mention her last name. But anyway, I told him there wasn't anyone named Gwen living in this house."

"And?"

"And then he asked me about the baby. And I lied to him. I told him that Eleanor was *my* baby. And that you were—my husband." The last two words were said softly, almost beneath her breath—to which Jeb Lacey paid not the slightest attention.

"And then he said he was looking for this Gwen woman because she had been indicted in Florida for kidnapping a baby. And what do you think about that?"

"As little as possible," Jeb retorted. "I don't doubt the truth of the story—well, part of the story. But I don't give a tinker's damn for the rest of it."

"How—do you mean that? He could come along with some police and arrest us both, couldn't he?"

"If he had a warrant he could. No warrant, no arrest. He's probably wiring his headquarters about that now."

"But they *could* arrest us?"

"Anything's possible," he said, "but they'd have to arrest us here in Virginia, and then extradite us to Florida, if the state of Virginia agreed. And one of the things a busy writer does—— Are you listening, Meg?"

"I'm listening."

"So let's take that tear out of your eye." He leaned over toward her again and whipped a handkerchief from the pocket of his shorts. "One of the things a busy writer does," he continued, "is to maintain a good lawyer—the best he can find—to protect him from plagiarism, slander, and—stealing babies."

"But he—sounded so sure of himself. And then he went over to the library, and if he grills the librarian he'll learn every possible bit of gossip in or about this town, and——"

"And there's nothing a detective agency hates worse than to get its name in a novel, good or bad. And a detective himself is always very careful not to get his name associated with something like that. Did you get his name?"

"I—never thought of that."

"And he went over to the library?"

She nodded.

"So you take care of the baby and I'll step across the street and see if I can find out something more. And don't, for goodness' sakes, cry any more. Eleanor does enough crying for both of us!"

She watched him as he slipped into shoes, buttoned his shirt, slipped on a sweater, and headed out the door. Rex followed him, whined when he was shut in, and lay on the front-door rug with his muzzle adjacent to the letter slot. I'd like to do that myself, Meg thought, but my nose could get caught. So instead she rushed to the front window and watched as her tall, thin hero went down to the sidewalk, swaggering like some ancient war hero, swinging his camera at his side. And then the baby started to cry again.

Millie McGruder was making closing noises as the library clock zeroed in on four-thirty. There was only one customer in the room. "Why, here's Mr Lacey now," she announced. The man at the far end of the room looked up quickly and ducked behind one of the shelves. But Millie would have none of that.

"That gentleman," she said to Jeb, "has spent half the day asking me questions about the Lacey family. I can't imagine just what it is he wants."

"Just suppose I try to find out," Jeb said as he turned and walked down between the shelves in the direction where the man had hidden. "Mr Pinkerton?"

The man stood up slowly. "All right, I was just making inquiries," he said angrily. Jeb brought his camera up and snapped three quick shots. The man pushed both hands up in front of his face. "Hey," he objected. "Cut that out."

"In case you don't know," Jeb said, "we have an organization that makes inquiries. We call it the police department. Now, unless you want to spend some time with our fine policemen, you'd better tell me what's going on. Starting with your name."

"Say, now, I'm a licensed private investigator. I have a license . . ."

"What you'll have in just a minute is a punch in the mouth from a man who doesn't care for private investigators. Show me your license."

"All right, all right. Don't get your bowels in an uproar." He reached into his pocket and pulled out a wallet. Jeb took it from him.

"Write this down for me, Millie," Jeb requested. Millie picked up her pen. "Anthony Rogers, Pinkerton Agency, Clearwater, Florida." He handed the wallet back. "That your real name?"

"Yes," Rogers replied grumpily. "You have no right to take my pictures like that."

"Hellfire," Jeb said. "Oh, excuse me, Miss Millie." He turned back to the detective. "The next thing I'm going to do is to publish your picture in all the local papers," he threatened. "Unless you tell me just what you're doing here."

"I'm—investigating."

"Investigating what?"

"I'm looking to find a woman by the name of Gwen Lacey."

"My sister," Jeb said. "She's living in Toronto. That's in Canada, in case you don't know. So what else is on your mind?"

"In Canada? Damn!"

"Damn is right. Isn't this strange?"

Evidently Rogers found nothing strange or desirable about his predicament. He glared at Jeb as if trying to ruin him, the way the Israelites did at the walls of Jericho.

"You know, of course," Jeb continued, "that Pinkerton has an office in Richmond, not thirty-five miles away from here. So tell me, why would a branch office in Clearwater, Florida send an agent all the way up here to—investigate?" Rogers took a deep breath, almost seeming to choke himself. "Or perhaps it's a private case?" Jeb prompted.

"Yes, yes," he agreed. "A private case. Confidential."

"Of course," Jeb said. "A private case. In other words, Rogers, you're a bounty hunter!"

A moment of silence.

"Now, suppose we discuss just *why* you're looking for my sister Gwen."

"Well, I——"

"You told my wife that you had a fugitive warrant. Is that true?"

"Your wife?"

"My wife. As in family, child, mother, wife. Well, show me your warrant."

"I—don't have a warrant."

"In other words, you lied?"

"Well, PIs have to shade the truth sometimes in order to get the facts, you know."

"No, I don't know," Jeb said. "I don't much believe in stretching the truth. But I'll tell you what. I write novels for a living——"

"Oh, yes, he does," Millie interrupted. "Hundreds of them. All interesting."

"And widely read," Jeb said. "So, Mr Rogers, tomorrow I'm going uptown to talk to my good friend the chief of police. And if I find you inside the city limits of Urbanna again you can expect that I'll do a few unpleasant things, including, by the way, writing a story for the *New York Times* about what a lousy service Pinkerton, and particularly you, Mr Rogers, provide to the public. And I might also put you in one of my murder stories—as the villain, of course. Do you read me?''

''I'm only trying to make a living,'' Rogers grumbled.

''So am I,'' Jeb retorted. ''Now, you get the picture? Out of town by tomorrow at sunrise, or else. And just in case you can't remember that long I'll be telephoning your Clearwater branch office at nine tomorrow morning, and you can be sure I'll have a lot of interesting things to be said about you.''

Rogers backed off a step or two. His belligerent look was fading fast.

''All right,'' he muttered. ''I'm going.''

Jeb tugged at the investigator's necktie. ''Nice piece of work,'' he said. ''The door's over there. Be on your way.''

Rogers tucked his license back into his pocket. ''One day you might be sorry,'' he threatened.

''One day I might,'' Jeb agreed. ''But you've already reached *your* day.'' With one hand he grabbed the man's shoulder and pushed him to the door. Millie hustled in front of them to open it.

''Glad you could come, Mr Rogers,'' she said sweetly. ''We always welcome researchers, at any time.''

''The hell you say,'' Rogers remarked as he was propelled out the door.

''My, wasn't that exciting?'' Mrs McGruder said. ''I do so admire forceful men.''

"I appreciate that," Jeb said, "but I'm newly married, and you mustn't let my wife hear you say that."

"Of course," Millie responded, giggling. "It will be our secret!"

CHAPTER FOUR

MEG HUBBARD was standing by the door as he came up the walk, whistling. She held the door open for him, and backed Rex away so Jeb could squeeze in.

"You're whistling. So we don't have to go to jail?"

"Never a chance," he told her as he picked her up and whirled her in a circle around him. "Never a chance. The guy turns out to be a fake, working on a private case. He wants Gwen, not us."

"Well, thank the Lord for that. He'll never find her unless somebody tells him."

"Yes."

"You didn't? You did!"

"Why should we share all the worry?"

"But she's your sister!"

"You keep saying that," Jeb said. "If you'd had a sister like Gwen you might feel different about it." He gave her another whirl. Rex barked at the excitement, and woke up the baby.

"Put me down, you big ox!" He stopped the whirling, but kept her captive, some six inches above the floor.

"Big ox?"

"I—perhaps spoke too sharply," she said nervously. No matter how well she might know him he was a giant of a man who might—who might do all sorts of things! "Put me down—please."

"That's what I like in a woman—gentility, prudence, subservience."

The moment her heels grounded on the floor she yelled at him and threatened with both fists.

"Gentility, subservience, hell! One more conversation like that and I'm going to pound your head into a square, damn you."

"Ah, I'm glad your grandmother can't hear that," he said, shaking his head dolefully. "And the baby?"

She backed off a step or two, hands on hips, her face red with anger and her golden hair swinging back and forth across her face. "Why is it that you don't seem worried a bit?" she demanded. "That baby belongs somewhere to somebody, and you can bet they've got all the law they can find trying to locate her. Maybe this Pinkerton is a fake, but sooner or later some real cops are going to come down the pike. And then what, *Mr* Lacey?"

"You don't have to worry about a thing," he said, grinning down at her. "The baby was here in the house when you came, right?"

Meg nodded.

"So nobody can accuse *you* of kidnapping. And you can't be made to testify against *me*."

"How do you figure that?"

"Easy. Just as soon as any authority shows up at the front door we're out the back. We go up the street, find a preacher and get married. A wife can't be made to testify against her husband. How about that?"

"I don't know what about that," Meg said fretfully. "But it'll make Gran very happy!"

"Now that's a thought," he said, chuckling. "Maybe Gran would stand up with you?"

All this time Meg was gradually losing her temper again. "And just what makes you think I'd marry you just to keep you out of jail?"

"You wouldn't do it for me?"

"Probably not."

"Nor for the baby?"

"Oh, get off my back," she muttered. "It's been a hard hard day. At the moment I'd feel better running off to a convent instead of marrying you!"

"What a blow that would be," he said sadly as he squeezed his way into his favorite chair in front of the computer.

"Don't give me that, Jeb Lacey," she snapped. "You're a ham actor almost as much as you're a ham writer. Why don't you go back to *The Devil Duke* before you cry all over the house?"

"You know," he said slowly, "you might have the right idea. I believe I will. Now, where was I?"

"You left the Duke in bed with the Duchess of Wrantham, and her husband had just driven up to the door. I hope Wrantham challenges him to a duel to the death and then turns the Duchess out into the street."

"No, that wouldn't do for a Regency romance," Jeb said, sighing. "The Duchess couldn't make a living on the streets. Noble prostitutes were not the thing in England in 1804. I'm afraid you don't have the right viewpoint for romance."

"Do you blame me, sharing a house with you?"

"Now, Meg, that's no way to talk. Did you feed the baby?"

"No, I didn't. It's your niece, not mine. I need more information for my article. When did you write your first book?"

"When I was sixteen, I think it was. But why should I tell you if you're not going to feed the baby?"

"So all right, I'll feed the baby. When did you write your first book?"

"When I was sixteen, I think it was."

"Dear lord," Meg groaned as she snatched up the baby and headed for the kitchen. A moment later she called back, "And my gran was probably right about you all along!"

But Jeb Lacey was already deep in the stews of old London, and could not be bothered by modern problems.

Silence settled over the house like the eve of the armistice at Verdun. It was an uneasy sort of quiet, broken now and again by the slap of the baby's spoon, or her little giggle. Eventually it came to be eight o'clock in the evening. There was a clean-up clatter in the kitchen, and Meg appeared at the foot of the stairs, the sweet-smelling child riding, giggling, on her hip.

"I'm not even going to say goodnight to you," Meg growled. "You don't deserve it. I'm going home to my gran's house tomorrow."

That snapped his head up out of his musing. "Going home to Gran? You can't do that!"

"And why not?"

"Because all Urbanna knows you've been living here with me and the baby. Your reputation is ruined."

"So who cares?" she said, snorting. "The longer I stay, the worse it gets. I might just as well quit while I'm ahead."

"Meg?"

But Meg had gone, zooming up the stairs on those long, shapely legs of hers, the baby enjoying every inch of the ride. Damn fool, he told himself. Where else could you find a better one than she? Her? Or a nicer baby, for a fact. It can't be Gwen's child; the kid is too nice to be the daughter of such a rotten woman. Don't you remember?

He remembered, of course. He was six years younger than his sister. On her tenth birthday she had pushed him off the second-story balcony into the prickly bayberry bushes. Result, one broken arm, one broken leg. His leg still bothered him on damp days. And when she was thirteen, and wanted to go sailing with that idiot Charlie Farrel, the pair of them had taken him out into the middle of the river and thrown him overboard. Luckily he could swim well enough to stay afloat until one of the oyster boats had picked him up.

And his mother, remember? "Oh, Gwen must only have been teasing you, Jeb. There's nothing serious to that!"

Except that it almost drowned him!

And now here he was, a neurotic fiction writer, doing exactly the same sort of thing to Meg Hubbard. His hand slapped down on the off switch on his computer, and he watched the green-colored words disappear into the black. There was quiet above his head, on the second floor. He slowly pushed his chair back from the keyboard and stood up. What to say? What to do?

He ran one hand through his hair. It wasn't as thick as it once had been. He rubbed a couple of times. Dandruff, for sure. And he thought of Meg's long golden plait. Full, bright, almost to her waist. And the baby, no hair at all at eight months, but a quadruple set of teeth, "all the better to bite you with," as the wolf said. Another front tooth had cut through this afternoon, and Meg had had a bottle of something that deadened the pain. "Gawd," he muttered as he pushed his chair away and went slowly up the stairs.

All the bedroom doors were open. A half-light gleam came from Meg's room, speckling the multicolored rug on the corridor floor. As quietly as a sneak-thief Jeb Lacey pussy-footed down the hall and peeped around the corner of the doorjamb. Eleanor was asleep in her big crib, all curled up like a kitten.

Meg sat in the upholstered chair under the floor lamp, holding a book in her hand, not reading—not even looking at the book—and crying. Jeb could feel his throat block up. Crying because of me? he wondered. He pulled his shoulders back and walked into the room.

"Meg?"

Her head snapped up and the book closed with a thump and fell to the floor.

"What do you want? Don't wake the baby."

"I won't." He walked over to her, picking up the book she had dropped and handing it back to her.

"I've been some kind of a pig," he said.

"Yes," she agreed. It gave him another shock. Most women he knew would have fumbled around with some sort of forgiveness statement, but not Meg Hubbard.

He fought back the urge to retaliate, to strike back. Instead he moved closer and put one hand on her shoulder. She was wearing the robe he had bought her. Gold. Silk and satin. Sexy smooth—and hard to hang on to.

"I'm sorry, Meg. I don't know why I picked on you. I think it was because I was—thinking of my sister. And the baby." There was a box of tissues beside her chair. He tugged one out and wiped her tears. She managed a trembling little smile. Not something that lasted a long time, but at least it was there for a moment, like a setting sun before it dipped below the horizon and was gone.

She dropped the book onto the chair. "Lacite Sanson," she said. "I never did care for her writing, but my grandmother thinks she's a marvelous author."

"Yes, I hear that there are people on both sides of the fence," he said. His voice was soft, caressing. She looked up at him, smiling, and moved closer, until his arm slipped over her shoulder and down her side.

"I suppose you've read all her works?" She cocked her head, brushing aside the burst of gold that shaded her face.

"I suppose I have," he returned, "but I can't say that I cared for any of them. Women writers, you know." And he didn't say a word about the fact that Lacite Sanson was one of his pseudonyms.

"Aha," she returned. "Masculine humors?"

"Probably. It isn't often that any but the superstars can appeal to both sexes." He increased the pressure of his arm, turning her tightly into his body and steering her toward the door. He directed her out into the corridor and down the hall to the double French windows that opened onto the second-floor balcony. One of the doors stuck.

"Wouldn't you know?" he complained as he struggled with it. "Just when I want to set up a romantic scene, the damn door sticks." She giggled at him, a soft low sound which she buried against his sweater. The wind gave a hand, snatching the door out of his hands and swinging it open.

It was a stronger wind than it had been earlier. He ushered her out onto the balcony. High clouds were racing eastward, out toward the river and the sea. Dark, fleeting clouds, hurrying to do some damage somewhere. She snuggled up against him for the warmth of sharing. He tightened his grip.

His hand slipped up an inch or two and took possession of her fulsome breast. For a fraction of a second she moved reflexively, and then settled back in position, leaving the field to him. Changed her mind? Jeb asked himself as he applied the slightest squeeze. But no. She sighed and said nothing. He moved another inch or two, dropping her zipper, leaving a space for penetration. She shivered uneasily. "Cold hands?" she asked.

"Warm heart," he responded as his hand slipped inside and rested authoritatively on her soft breast. It was like taking a handful of glory, this soft, easy movement. Her breast tightened against his fingers, her nipple rose tautly and became entangled between them— and the baby began to cry.

"Damn chaperon," he muttered in her ear, and kissed its tip.

"You've nobody to blame but yourself," she said, laughing. She backed away from him. His hand held on gently, dolefully, and then let her soft fullness slip away. His last touch re-did the zipper and the whole affair was gone, like a mirage in the desert. She reached up on tiptoes and kissed his nose before she ran.

He stood outside in the cool air for another few minutes as rain spat against the glass door beside him. Daydreams—or night dreams—a total recall of all that had happened. Such softness, such firmness. Think, idiot, he lectured; all you have to say is, Let's get married, and you could have that and everything else for— forever? Or at least a long time!

Growling at himself, he closed the French doors behind him and padded down the hall. Outside Meg's room he peered in. She was sitting in the big plush chair, holding Eleanor and her bottle. The babe was hard at work, making little noises as she sucked on her formula, kicking her little feet free from the blanket, thoroughly enjoying herself. And Meg was smiling out into the darkness— not particularly seeing anything, but just pleased with the way her life was advancing.

He moved into the dim light splashing out from her lamp, and she looked up from the child and smiled at him. Ask, he told himself. Ask or you'll never know. He crossed the threshold and walked over to the contented pair.

"When I first came in," he said, "you were crying... Why?" And his ears went up for the answer. Crying for him? Crying about him? Wanting him?

"Oh, that," she replied, and her eyes sparkled. "That was nothing. I was trying to hem the baby's nightgown and the needle stuck in my finger. I hate that."

"Me too," he said angrily, and stalked off to bed.

He tossed and turned half the night. Plots sparked through his mind. Realities did as well. Meg and I. Meg and me. Meg. Whatever it was, he was unable to fall asleep until after twelve o'clock. When the storm homed in on Urbanna in full strength it caused him to stir, but not much. But when the hand came down on his shoulder at two in the morning his eyes flashed open, took in the face of the clock, and then settled on the tall woman dressed in the plain white nightgown, standing by his bed. Automatically he shifted to the side of his double bed and threw back the covers.

"No," she said.

Both eyes came open; he squinted at her in the semi-darkness. Lightning flashed at the windows. He sat up, forgetting that he preferred to sleep in the altogether. "What?"

"The rain," she said. "The roof. Come help me move the baby's crib."

He bounced out of bed. Roofs and rain he understood, having lived in the house for a reasonable part of his life. Since he normally slept naked, he presented a sight to be seen. Meg backed off from him, one hand covering her mouth. She was *not* the most innocent virgin in the world; in fact she had known more than one or two men, to say the least. Not in the biblical sense, but not exactly casually, either.

But not men like this one. He was tall, of course, but, underneath all that sloppy clothing he was built to endure, she had never seen a man quite as—magnificent. She turned her back on him.

He made apologetic noises, and she could hear him scrambling for the clothing he had piled on the chair next to the bed. It took a moment or two, and then he joined her. "OK," he said. "Move the baby. Rain."

She turned around gratefully. "It really leaks, Jeb. Like a river, almost, and——"

"Not to worry. First we rescue the baby."

It's nice, Meg told herself, to have someone to follow in emergencies. Some nice man. And so she did—follow him, that was. He had managed to find a pair of old blue jeans, into which he could barely fit his muscular posterior, and an old sweater that sleekly followed his chest muscles.

They both rushed into the other bedroom. "You're right," he said. "It's coming down like a flood." But however it was coming down it had hardly bothered Eleanor. Now, though, with the pair of them at her bedside making conversation, the baby awoke, just at the moment that a large-scale drop of water fell directly onto her nose. And she filed a protest. Loudly. Meg ducked under the deluge and swept the child up in her arms.

"Nothing we can do here," Jeb told her. "Take the kid back to my room. I'll see if I can move the crib, and in the meantime maybe you could—do something?"

Meg was gone in a moment, and back in another. "I left her wrapped up in your bed," she explained. "You'll need help in moving that crib."

"Not worth the effort," he said. "Everything's soaked, from mattress to blankets to spring to—nuts. I'm going down to bring up the playpen. That ought to take care of her for the rest of the night."

He went ambling off down the stairs. Playpen, Meg thought. It would never have crossed my mind. Not ever. She collapsed on her own bed and then sprang up with a little shriek. Her bed was wetter than the baby's crib. She met Jeb as he came back upstairs. "The whole room is soaked," she complained. "My bed is soaked. The floor is soaked. The rug is soaked."

"Now that," Jeb said, "makes a problem." He struggled sidewise into the room with the collapsible playpen under his arm. Just in time. For Baby Eleanor had come free from her blanket-trap, rolled over twice to the edge of his bed, and was about to dive off onto the floor. Jeb dropped the playpen and made a dive for the baby. The playpen landed first. He landed on top of it, his arms outstretched, and the baby came down in third place, safe and sound in his arms. And of course, being a true female, she giggled.

Jeb managed to sit up. Meg stood just at the door, not sure whether to come in or stay out. "Come on," he grumbled. "Take the kid."

"She's not a kid," Meg said. "Did you hurt yourself?"

"If I didn't," he muttered, "it was no thanks to you. Gawd. I think I landed on my—next to the hinges."

"But the baby's safe and sound," Meg said cheerfully as she bounced Eleanor up and down. "Now what do we do?"

"If my back isn't broken I'm going to get up," he said as he rolled over on his stomach and got his knees underneath him. "And the first female that laughs gets it. You get it?"

"I get it," Meg said, smothering a smile which was entirely too excessive. Jeb struggled to his feet.

"Now, then," he said as he reached for the overhead light. "How do you unfold this damned playpen?"

"Why don't you hold the baby and let me do this?" Meg offered. "We used to have half a dozen of these at the church for use by the congregation."

"You mean to tell me you know about this sort of thing?"

"I mean to tell you I know about this." She handed over the child, dried her hands on the sides of her nightgown, and fell to the struggle. In minutes the bottom of the playpen fell in with a thump, and the latch closed. "Now, if we only had a blanket..." she mused.

"Take one off my bed," Jeb ordered.

Minutes passed. Eleanor squirmed in her new nest, and then closed both eyes. That was all it took.

"Well, thank the Lord for that," Meg said. "Now all we have to do is take care of me, right?"

"That's right," Jeb assured her. "Only——"

"Only? You must have a dozen rooms in this house."

"Eleven," Jeb told her. "That's not the problem."

"Oh? Why am I so suspicious of you, Jeb Lacey?"

"I can't imagine." There could certainly not be any more innocent soul in all of Urbanna than Jeb Lacey— at least from the sound of him.

"So there's a 'yes, but'," she said firmly. "Tell me what it is."

"Did you know that the—er—back of your nightgown is wet?" he asked.

"I know. My bed is soaked. I sat down on it. Now, what's the problem?"

"The problem is—you wouldn't believe."

"I'll believe. Get to it."

Jeb took a deep breath and talked as fast as his tongue would go. "The problem is that although I have plenty of rooms I don't have any other beds—and only a couple of extra blankets!"

"Aha," Meg said. "You've gone to all this trouble just to get me in your bed?"

"Well, I didn't arrange the rain storm, nor the hole in the roof, but as it happens my bed is the only bed available. There's plenty of room. Two of us could sleep together with no trouble at all."

"You must think I came down in yesterday's rain storm," she told him. "What sort of woman do you think I am?"

"I don't know, but I'm willing to find out," he returned. "So I'll tell you what we'll do."

"You have that a little confused," Meg said. "Now *I'll* tell *you* what we're going to do. First of all, it's almost three o'clock, nearly the time you would be going downstairs to work on your latest book. *The Devil Duke*, I believe?"

"You don't mean——"

"Yes, I *do* mean. You may go downstairs. You can get to work on your book, or you can stretch out on the couch, or——"

"That's a mighty small couch," he complained.

"Ah, but think of all the work you can get done," she said. "And in the meantime I'll camp out on your bed and keep watch over the baby. Right?"

"It doesn't seem exactly fair," Jeb muttered. But then he saw the look on her face. "All right, all right, I'm going."

"Here. I'm not the hard-hearted woman that you think." She whipped another blanket from his bed and stuffed it in his stomach. "Goodnight, lover."

"Spoilsport," he muttered, and wandered dolefully back down the stairs. Rex was waiting for him at the bottom. "Thrown out of my own bed and my own bedroom," he told the dog. Rex whined, considered the situation, and went back to his rug. It was a soft, fluffy rug, and there was no doubt that man's best friend was not about to share it with Jeb.

Shaking his head, Jeb went over to his computer, whipped out the chair, and slumped down into it. A touch of his fingers and *The Devil Duke* popped up at him. For a moment he just couldn't remember what the plot was all about. The Duchess of Wrantham?

His fingers tickled the keys, and the Duke began his seduction. The Duchess was soaking wet, and her nightgown clung to her as if it were a second skin. London was in an uproar. The guns were thundering at Waterloo...and Jeb Lacey lifted his head from where it had been resting on top of his computer monitor. The rain had stopped, the morning sun was shining weakly through the study windows, and somebody was banging on the front door.

He struggled to his feet. The thundering stopped for a moment, and then continued again. The only thing available to him was a bottle of cognac, sitting half-empty on the side table. He wandered over to it, plucked out the cork, and took a deep decent drink. Back to the front door. With only one eye open he managed the lock and pulled the door open.

Sergeant Hergerman of the State Police stood on his doorstep. He was an elderly man, well known to Jeb because of his interest in detective fiction. The sergeant looked as if he had been up all night. And so do I, Jeb thought.

"You got a woman here?" the cop asked.

"I got two women here," Jeb returned. "Is it against the law?"

"Probably. The way you do it, probably. You got a woman by the name of Meg Hubbard here?"

"I got one of them," Jeb returned. "Is *that* against the law?" .

"Smart I don't need," the sergeant returned. "The rescue squad just took her grandmother to the Rappahannock General Hospital. Heart attack."

"Come in, come in," Jeb said. "Meg's here. I'll get her!" His feet were running before his mouth had stopped. Up the stairs, two at a time, with Rex following close behind, barking his fool head off.

Meg was already up, awakened by the noisy call, wrapped in her golden robe. Baby Eleanor was awake as well, sprawled out in her playpen, kicking away, clothed in diaper and baby shirt.

"Meg," he said urgently. "It's your grandmother. They've taken her to the Rappahannock General. Get yourself dressed. We'll take the baby with us. My car is out back, and we have a police escort waiting."

* * *

Rappahannock General Hospital was unfortunately on the other side of the river. They bounced down to Route Three and over the Robert Opie bridge, close up behind the speeding police car. By the time they arrived at the Emergency entrance Gran Hubbard had already been examined and sent down for a heart procedure. Dr Switzer was a busy man, but he took a few minutes to talk to them. Jeb bounced Baby Eleanor on his knee while the conversation went on.

"Heart blockage," the little surgeon said. "We don't know how bad it may be. We have her downstairs now while they run a catheter procedure to find out. There's no need for tremendous alarm, but I'm sure you recognize that at her age crossing the highway is a danger. Now, if you two will sit down here while we get some background information...?"

Both Jeb and Meg were still groggy from lack of sleep. They fell into a pair of the lounge chairs in the waiting room. Eleanor started feeding almost immediately. A nursing aide came in with a form sheet about ten miles long, and the inquisition began. Not until they reached the insurance section did the conversation get pressing.

"Medicare, you realize, will not cover all the expenses," the aide said. "Do you have an ancillary insurance?"

"Not that I know of," Meg said anxiously. "Does that mean we——?"

"It doesn't mean a thing," Jeb said. "My mother-in-law, you know." He pulled out an engraved card from his wallet and passed it over. "I'll pay all the ancillary expenses out of my own pocket. Would you like a check now?"

"That's not necessary," the aide replied, "but you should be aware that the costs could run up to thousands of dollars."

"No problem," Jeb said. "Give her the best of everything. Private room, Meg?"

"I don't think so," Meg said. "You know how she loves to talk. If there's nobody to talk to she might feel very bad." The surgeon nodded, the aide smiled and the administrator who had come to join them grinned from ear to ear.

"Mr Lacey? Of *Desperation in the Dust*? Fine book. I sat up all one night reading it! Fine book."

"It kept me up all one night too," Jeb confided. And at that moment the internist came in, shedding his greens. "Three tubes blocked," he reported. "We can't clear them with the catheter."

Meg turned white. Even the baby stopped her giggles. "That means?" Meg asked.

"That means I have to go up to the operating room," the surgeon said. "Now listen carefully. We have to perform an operation. It's called open-heart surgery, but despite the name it's being done thousands of times in hundreds of American hospitals, and has become as routine as baking apple pie. So I don't want you to be too worried about the affair. We'll do the operation immediately, and you both can sit here and play with the baby for about four hours. Or two of you could go back home and leave just one on guard duty over us..."

"Not to worry, he says," Meg murmured. "I'll damn well worry if I want to. Why don't you go home and get the roof fixed?"

"Yes, and order a few more beds and things," Jeb added. "You sure you'll be all right?"

"I'm sure. But I promised my editor the second section of my article. It's on the computer. Could you...?"

"Of course I could," he said as he leaned over and kissed her enthusiastically. The surgeon grinned.

"Newly-weds," Jeb explained. "Can't afford to have mother-in-law problems this early in our married life."

Meg clung to him, bringing her lips up to his ear. "Jeb Lacey," she whispered, "you are the darnedest liar I ever met. Newly-weds!" A tear ran down her cheek. "There are times," she whispered, "when I wish it were so."

"And while I'm arranging things," he returned, "maybe I could arrange that too. Here. You might need this."

Out of his loose jacket pocket he pulled a handful of crumpled twenty-dollar bills and pushed them into her hands.

"Oh, Lord, that's too much," she gasped. One-handed, the other holding the baby, he unsnapped her purse and wadded the bills into it.

"Don't you believe it," he said. "You're in a hospital. A cup of coffee would cost you a mint, and Lord knows what it'll be for a luncheon sandwich."

"Jeb Lacey, you are one fine guy," she told him, and burst into tears.

"You know," he said as the nursing aide led her out to the OR waiting room, "I'm beginning to believe that myself!"

Baby Eleanor crowed in delight. She already knew just what kind of a man he was.

CHAPTER FIVE

ANNIE MAE HUBBARD came home from the hospital twenty days later, riding luxuriously in the air-conditioned back seat of Jeb Lacey's Cadillac. Home to the house on Virginia Street, that was, not to her old house out on Kent Street. Sultry summer was gone; cool October was here.

"Because," Meg tried to explain, "you have to have someone with you, Gran. You can't just live by yourself. Besides, you'll like Jeb's house—if the roof is fixed?"

"All fixed," Jeb said. "Practically a new roof, to tell the truth."

"But all my friends..." Annie Mae said. "And my garden." But as Jeb drove the car down Virginia Street and up the drive she changed her mind somewhat. "Why, it's the old customs house!" she exclaimed. "Why, I— for a little while it might be OK."

"Whatever you think," Jeb told her gently. "When you decide you want to go back to your *real* house we'll hire a lady to come live with you."

Annie Mae's lips puckered up and quivered. "No need for that," she said. There was a wobbly sound to her voice, a sound of imminent tears. "When I'm ready to go Meg can come with me."

"Not possible," Jeb said softly. "Meg is staying here with me—and our baby."

"But—but you can't do that," Annie Mae complained. "You're not even married, you two."

79

"Here we go now." Jeb slid out of the front seat of the car, opened the back door, and lifted Annie Mae up as if she were fifty pounds of turnip greens. Meg, hurrying in front of them, turned the wheelchair around to welcome them.

"An electric wheelchair?" she queried. "You didn't have to be all that fancy."

"You hush, girl," Annie Mae said. "Let the man make his own decisions."

"Your grandmother tried out several different chairs at the hospital," Jeb explained, "and the one she liked best was the electric model."

"He's really a nice man," Annie Mae assured her granddaughter. Both of them stared at her for her sudden change of mind. And then Annie Mae said dolorously, "If only you were married it would be perfect."

"He's already perfect," Meg said. "Who's got the baby?"

"Oops. I believe we left her asleep in the back seat of the car," Jeb said. "Somebody overlooked her."

"Your job," Meg told him. "I have the grandmother, you have the baby."

"What a nice division of labor," he said, *sotto voce*.

"You're really not all *that* nice," Meg murmured. "There's a lot of improvement could be made."

"I don't see how," Jeb responded proudly. "Take your grandmother into the house."

"I don't have the key," she said.

"You don't need the key. Just ring the bell."

So she did. One lusty ring on the old bell and the door opened. A middle-aged black man—a very large man—held it wide and smiled at her. "Mrs Lacey? Welcome home."

Meg had expected a problem getting the wheelchair over the threshold, but it failed to materialize. The threshold was gone. The chair went smoothly across the space where it once had been, and the dull paper that had made the hall so gloomy was gone as well.

"Nice," Annie Mae said. "Most hallways in this town are as dull as dishwater. Who's he?"

"Jeb?" Meg turned around. He came bounding up the stairs, carrying the baby in his outstretched hands. Eleanor was laughing gleefully. "Who's he?" she muttered, nodding toward the man at the door.

"Oh, that's Otis Dixon," Jeb said. "He's the fellow who's to butle for us."

"Butle?"

"You know, a butler. Answers the door and the telephone, tells my sister that there's nobody home, supervises the maid and the cook. Like that."

"Hooee," Meg said, startled. "How we have come up in the world! With a maid and a cook?"

"How else? We need witnesses."

"I'm sure we do," she said, looking around her suspiciously. "Witnesses for what?"

"For the wedding."

"For the——"

"Wedding. It's not a hard word if you put your mind to it."

"But——"

"No buts," Jeb said. "I'll just have to write a little faster, that's all."

Dixon came out from the study with a tiny cellular telephone in hand. Jeb held up both hands in a stop signal. "Not my sister?"

"A gentleman by the name of Saul," Dixon said. "Saul Berkowitz."

"My agent," Jeb told them all as he took the telephone. "Annie Mae, why don't you cruise around the house for a look? Mrs Brill is in the kitchen, and our maid is upstairs making up beds."

"That's a relief," Meg said. "Beds? Plural?"

"Plural," he confirmed. "One bed in every one of the eleven rooms upstairs."

"But Gran——"

"We've converted two of the downstairs living rooms for her. Twelve beds. Is my arithmetic all that bad?"

"Not at all," Meg told him as she stretched to kiss his cheek. "There are times when even I think you're sweet. Come on, Gran, let's look around."

"Agents," Gran said. "I think I'd rather listen to what agents say. I've never met an agent—except for the insurance agent we used to have when you were small, Meg. I never did like him! He was as crooked as a snake's belly."

"Nosy Parker," Meg muttered.

"I heard that," Annie Mae almost shouted. "I heard that! Look at me. I'm alive and healthy. And curious." She gave her granddaughter an artificial smile. "And naturally I'm interested in what goes on in this marvelous house."

"Must be nice to your elders," Jeb chided, and then stepped out of the way of the sharp elbow that Meg directed toward him. "Saul! What can I do for you?" There was a pause. "Uh-huh," Jeb said. Another pause. "You don't say!" And again a long listen. "Well, I'll be darned!"

Another pause. "Well, thank you, Saul. I find it almost unbelievable. Yes, Carlotta was inserted by my wife. Drawn just like her, too." And he flicked the switch and handed it back to the butler.

"Well?" Annie Mae demanded.

"My agent says that our last book, *Murder in Moldavia*, has been selected by the Detective Book Club. He especially likes the heroine, Carlotta—says she's not as artificial as most of my women."

"Wonderful," Meg cried, clapping her hands. Dixon smiled; the baby cooed. Then Meg sobered. "Your *wife* gave you the character Carlotta?"

"What's that mean?" Annie Mae demanded.

"More money," Jeb said. "A lot more money."

"I didn't mean that," Annie Mae said stubbornly. "I mean what does that 'my wife' mean? Are you already married? Is that why——?"

"Gran!"

"Well, I want to know. How else do I find out anything if I don't ask questions?"

"You have a right to know," Jeb said. "No, I'm not married, but my agent thinks I am. I find it better for business if people think I'm married."

"But you're not?"

"But I'm not. Satisfied?"

"For the moment," Annie Mae said. "For the moment."

"So why don't we run along and let Jeb talk to his agent in private?" Meg suggested.

"I like agents," Annie Mae declared. "Does he call every month?"

"Not hardly," Meg said. "Come on, Gran, that's the end of the show. Let's go see the house."

They had their first real argument after supper that night. Annie Mae had gone to sleep by seven o'clock. Baby Eleanor had conked out by seven-thirty. And by that same hour Mrs Brill had cooked and cleaned, Gertrude washed and went, Dixon butled and beat it, and Meg came out to the study, pulling up a chair next to Jeb and said, "All right, let's have it out now."

"Have it out?" Jeb's fingers were poised half an inch above the keyboard, and remained there in total suspension. "Have what out?"

"You know what. Why do we have all this discussion about marriage? You're sending Gran over the hills with enjoyment. But I know darn well you no more want to get married now than we did three weeks ago. Remember the permanent bachelor bit?"

"I can't say that I do," he drawled.

"Well, I remember it right well, Mr Lacey. Starting from day number one it's been no marriage for you, until today, when all of a sudden it's been wedding bells and sweet music. And I don't like it!"

"You don't like the idea of marriage?"

"That's my gran's idea, not mine. I know you're trying to be a nice guy, but there's no need to go as far as *that*. When I—if I get married, it'll be because I love somebody and he loves me. No halfway ideas will do. No substitutions. No marriages of convenience. In a word, no!"

"My goodness. Them's pretty strong sentiments, lady. Surely I must have said *something* nice about marriage?"

"Oh, yes. *Said* something. From about the first night, when you were so eager to get me into your bed. No, thank you."

"No, you still don't want to come to bed with me, or no, you still don't want to marry me? Don't you remember what I said about us and getting married if the Federal Bureau of Investigation showed up?"

"Oh, that. You were only making that up. The FBI aren't going to come around to our—your house looking for a stolen baby. Not after all this time."

"But if they do, you plan to throw me to the wolves? And me going out of my way to be good to Annie Mae. Do you call that friendly?"

"I don't know what to call that. Suspicion—maybe that's the word for it. I just suspicion you, Jeb Lacey."

"Those are fierce words," he said solemnly. "I had planned to go over to the Methodist Church tomorrow and make some arrangements. Are you telling me now that I ought not to go?"

"No. I mean yes. I mean—lord, I just don't know, do I? Why do you continually tie me up in knots, Jeb Lacey?"

"It's not something I plan for every day," he said somberly. "I had thought that we would have arrived at an agreement by now. Well, if we haven't we haven't. Do we still have our basic agreement? You get to write an article about me, providing you help look after the baby?"

"Yes, I'll stick to the agreement—well, there has to be a temporary addition. I'll take care of the baby if you'll help me take care of Annie Mae—and help me write the article."

He grinned at her and shook his head slowly. "Doesn't exactly seem to be an iron-clad contract," he said, "but yes, I'll add Annie Mae to the list of my new dependants. For a limited time, of course."

"Of course," she said softly, and stood up to leave. He moved back to his keyboard, and then held off as he caught the confused expression on her face.

"I can tell you one thing," she said, sighing. "If I ever do think of getting married, you can have first dibs."

"First what?"

"First dibs. First chance. Don't you know anything?"

"You Virginians sure do talk funny," he said, but there was a twinkle in his eye. And then his fingers dropped to the keyboard, and Meg knew his mind had moved elsewhere. She leaned over his brooding face and kissed him again, once, lightly, on the tip of his nose. His fingers flew. The Devil Duke was entering his carriage, headed for—the Lord only knew where, and Baby Eleanor was making crying noises from upstairs. Meg looked down at Jeb again, and, conscience nagging, headed for the stairs.

Jeb came upstairs just before midnight. The old house was settling, creaking and groaning in the wind. But all the people, except for himself and Rex, were long fast asleep. Too restless to sleep, he turned on his bed light and picked up the book he had been trying to read for the past four months. Like many authors he found reading someone else's work just a tad boring. One of the large wooden shutters on some window was not fastened securely, and a storm was approaching.

Determined to settle the problem, Jeb struggled into his robe and padded out into the corridor. The noise was coming from the far end of the hall. He started in that direction, pausing long enough to look into the room where Meg and the baby were asleep. A tiny night-light shed a little glow. Just enough to see the pair of them. Eleanor was out from under her blankets again, her tiny head butting up against the corner of the crib. There was a little touch of pink on her head.

Meg was stretched out flat on her back, her legs flung wide, barely covered by her cotton nightgown, her left hand coiled deep in her loose hair, her right hand cupped to cover the delightful breast which had escaped the bodice of her gown. A tiny smile flickered at the corners of her mouth.

How about that? he thought, his eyes eating her up. I could just—no, I couldn't either! He disciplined his wild-storming imagination and turned away toward the crib. Somebody had tied a little pink ribbon in Eleanor's hair—and I hadn't even noticed she had that much hair, he told himself. Real hair. Not all that much, of course, but real hair! And he knew from experience, having looked after the baby while Meg had spent several days at the hospital, that there were now six little teeth in that mouth, sharp as daggers!

Time to go. Softly. He re-settled the baby's blanket without stirring the child, and headed back to the door. He didn't even notice that one of Meg's big green eyes was open, tracking him across the room.

One of the French windows at the end of the hall was the guilty culprit. Someone had missed fastening the latch. He turned the handle and was about to re-fix the door when outside movement caught his attention.

It was storm-dark outside the window that looked out over Jamison's Cove, to the eastward, in the direction of the Rappahannock River. Storm-dark but not so dark that one could not see the little grey rubber boat that was making its way toward the old customs house landing. Or the two men who were in that boat, huddled down against the rain.

Something soft rubbed against Jeb's bare leg. "Down, Rex," he muttered. But it wasn't the dog that giggled and pressed against his shoulder. "Meg?"

"I couldn't sleep. And you couldn't either?"

"That's right. Guilty conscience or too much oyster stew."

"It couldn't have been the stew. I made that myself. What are you staring at?"

"Look directly ahead out there," he said. "That little boat. Do you see it?"

"Funny place for a boat," she agreed. "Shallow water, with no real entry point. How in the world did they get it into the cove?"

"Damned if I know," he returned, "but I'm about to find out." He closed the French door and started for the stairs. She gripped his arm with both hands.

"No," she said. "It could be dangerous. Don't go out there alone."

He shook his arm loose. "Stay here with the baby," he instructed. "I'm going downstairs to the rifle rack. After that I'm going to call the police."

"It's dangerous, Jeb."

"Maybe. But look, there's only one way to get into the cove by water, and that's under the Virginia Street bridge. It's a rubber boat, though. They might have carried it over the bluffs at Cross Street or the area around Fort Nonsense. In any event, girl, there's only one place it could be heading, and that's right for the old customs house landing. And that means right for this house. Now, things aren't the way they used to be. There are four people in this house, and I'm responsible for all of them. So while I go downstairs to make sure your grandmother is OK you go baby-sit. And keep your head down."

"And that's an order, I suppose?"

"You're darned right it is," he said.

"You men are all alike," she said. "You just have to give orders—and I suppose you expect all us women to jump to the command!"

"You ain't whistlin' Dixie," he muttered, and was gone down the stairs before she could squeeze in another objection.

"Damn man," she whispered, and shuddered, as if a cold wind were blowing down her front. "Damn man." But she was glad he was available. Much of the time he annoyed her. On the other hand, rubbing against the strength of him was a new kind of pleasure. She had known a man or two, but none was like Jeb Lacey. None had ever attracted her in the way that he did. Maybe, she thought, I was a fool for yelling at him earlier today. It could be—nice to be married to him, and I blasted him out for even suggesting it. Meg Hubbard, you are one foolish woman!

She folded her arms across herself, and turned back to peer out the French doors. The little boat was almost out of sight, close up against the rickety wharf not more than three dozen feet away from the house. Meg Hubbard is a tough little lady, she told herself, who can handle her share of trouble. That was the moment that Baby Eleanor let out a little complaint. Glad to hear it, Meg ran for the bedroom, plucked the child out of the crib, and walked the floor with her.

"There's safety in numbers," she whispered to the baby, "especially if one of the numbers is a big man!" Eleanor made no comment. She wanted a few drops of her formula, but Meg was no fool, and would not for love nor money go downstairs until Jeb called her.

Jeb, downstairs, was not all that sure about the world. He called the police station. Urbanna's police force was comparable to Urbanna's population—just enough to go around. "Stay inside and lock all the doors and windows," the cop instructed. "I'll have somebody over there pretty soon."

"Pretty soon?"

"That's what I said. Pretty soon. And lock the doors."

"You better believe it," Jeb muttered as he unlocked his gun rack and took out his double-barreled shotgun. "Just let 'em try to break in here," he told Rex. And for a moment he believed it—until he remembered that he hadn't bought a box of shells in a dog's age. "I wonder how soon pretty soon is?" he said to the dog. And Rex, having no idea about things like that, woofed gently, coiled himself up on his rug, and went to sleep.

"What was that?" The feeble call came from Annie Mae, from her strange new bedroom in her strange new house.

Jeb checked the locks on the door, put his shotgun down on the kitchen table, and padded into Gran's room. "Only me, Gran," he called. "I thought I heard you calling for something."

"What a good boy you are," she said. "I don't remember everything—but I surely wish I had a drink of water."

"No problem," he assured her. "Ice water or plain?"

"I do so prefer ice," she said. "What a good man you are, Jeb Lacey. Did I wake you up and all?"

"Not a bit, Annie Mae. I was downstairs working."

"On a new book? What kind?"

"A Regency romance," he said. "It's called *The Devil Duke*."

Annie Mae shivered with excitement. "Oh, my, I'd love to read that."

"And so you shall, just as soon as I get it finished," he promised. "Ice water, right?"

But when he came back she was already fast asleep. So he drank the water for himself, spent a few minutes in the downstairs bathroom, picked up his shotgun, and sat down in his computer chair to wait for whatever might come next. And that was where Meg and Eleanor found him at six the next morning, snoring away at thirteen to the dozen, his shotgun on the floor beside him and his dog lying across his feet, keeping him warm.

It was the smell of bacon that woke him. Bacon and eggs and country sausage, with coffee and toast and orange juice, all tastefully arrayed on two portable tables, one on either side of him.

"Well, what's all this?" he asked the empty air. Meg came in from the kitchen, Baby Eleanor on her hip.

"Breakfast," she said. "What else could we do after you spent the night protecting us?"

"Er—yes." He squinted with one eye closed just to see if she was pulling his leg. But she wasn't. She believed the whole ball of wax.

"Yes," he acknowledged. "It was a long night. Two men in the boat, and the police, and then Gran woke up and needed a glass of water. All in all a busy time. And how are my two ladies?"

Eleanor looked at him worshipfully. But then, he told himself, she always does that. Meg, who never did any of that worship stuff, smiled sweetly at him as if she was about to—worship, that was. He gave Rex a little nudge to get the dog off his bare feet. Just in case one of them might want to carry the worshiping a little further—to foot-kissing, perhaps. But that was asking too much, apparently.

He reached for the food plate. "Country sausages!" He smacked his lips. "My favorite breakfast food." It wasn't really. He preferred pancakes and maple syrup, but there was no need for Meg to know that. And for the first time in his adult life he felt a twinge of conscience at the lie.

"Eat up," she ordered. "Clean the plate."

"Oh, I will indeed. Every scrap. After all the time and effort you put into getting it ready. I'd have to——"

"Oh, I didn't cook it," Meg interrupted. "Mrs Brill came in early and made it all up. Including the baby's formula. Wasn't that nice? *Mangia*!"

"*Mangia?*"

"That's Italian for eat."

"*Mangia?* You speak Italian?"

"Of course. My other grandmother was Italian. Eat!"

And, knowing he was already on thin ice as a result of his police story—even in the middle of autumn—Jeb Lacey *mangiaed* with enthusiasm.

Lieutenant Overton of the police showed up at about eleven o'clock, accompanied by a plainclothes detective who never did get introduced. Overton shook hands with them both and then arched his eyebrows at Jeb.

"I would prefer to discuss this in private," Jeb said. "I wouldn't want the ladies to—well, you know. And Meg's grandmother is just back from the hospital after heart surgery. I wouldn't want her to even hear about the affair. Meg, would you leave us?"

"You really are a mean man," Meg pouted. "I'll bet the lieutenant doesn't chase his wife out of the room whenever there's an interesting story. Besides, I want you to look at this powder that your sister left."

"Look at powder?" Jeb shook his head. The two policemen hid their grins and nodded their sympathy.

"Contrarywise," Overton said, "I always chase my wife out before I have a discussion. Otherwise she'd be running the department. Something wrong with the baby powder?''

''Well, I don't have all that much experience,'' Meg said, frowning. ''This is our only child. But I thought baby powder was supposed to be fine and absorbent and smell sweet.''

''Well, there you go,'' Jeb said, reaching up for the can of powder. ''Take Eleanor out for a walk, go by the drugstore, and order whatever kind of powder you feel like having.''

''Bah, humbug,'' Meg said as she smiled at them all, picked up the baby, and walked out of the room. ''You're just looking for an excuse to get rid of me!'' The door slammed shut behind her with more enthusiasm than was necessary.

''And that's something I'd never tell my wife,'' the plainclothes policeman said. ''Go out and buy anything you like. Wow.''

''It doesn't apply,'' Overton said. ''Mr Lacey writes books. I suspect he makes as much in a week as we do in six months.''

Jeb, who was somewhat sensitive about the money he made, shrugged. ''Now what about these two men?'' he asked.

''Two men, yes.'' Overton pulled out his notebook and flipped through a page or two. ''Murphy and Jones. Young. Both from Washington.''

''State Department? FBI?'' Both of them burst out laughing.

''From one of the mobs,'' Overton said. ''They're so young that they don't know how to guard their mouths. We made an unfortunate mistake.''

Jeb's ears went up. ''An unfortunate mistake?''

"Yes. We picked them up just as they got out of the boat. Too soon. They hadn't done anything illegal at that time. They had a peculiar sort of package with them—a roll of little blankets. Baby blankets, I would guess. And all we've been able to get out of them is that you have something that belongs to them, and they were sent down to make you understand you couldn't get away with that."

"Let me get this straight. I have something that belongs to them? Good lord. The other guy wanted something to do with the baby. What in the world would I have that belongs to a bunch of gangsters?"

"Other guy?"

"A few weeks ago. He carried all the papers of a Pinkerton man. I gave him the quick heave-ho, and the next day I called the Pinkerton people, who claimed that they had no such operative. And now these people? They claim I have something that belongs to them?"

"Yes," Overton said. "They claim that——"

"Mr Lacey, could you let me see that box of powder?" his partner interrupted him.

"Why not?" Jeb tossed the can to him. He sniffed at it, touched a finger to the cap, and tasted. The lieutenant looked across at him, eyes raised.

"You *may* have something that belongs to them," he said. "But this isn't it. All you've got here is a box of adulterated talcum powder. Maybe a little sugar—or some sweetener—mixed in with it. Just where did you get this powder?"

Jeb Lacey had written too many books to miss the nuances, but he was not prepared to sell his sister down the river. Not without knowing something more than he did at the moment.

"All right," Jeb said. "What is it?"

"You write too many detective stories," the detective said, laughing. "Mind you, I've read more than a few of them and enjoyed them. But this stuff is not what you're thinking it is. It's baby powder—cheap baby powder, minus all the perfumes and absorbents in the more expensive stuff, but baby powder none the less."

"Well, thank God for that," Jeb said as he took his first good breath of the interview. After all, he thought, Gwen is my sister. Not too lovable, not too smart—but she's still my sister. "And there's no law against smuggling baby powder, I suppose?"

"None at all."

"Don't take this too casually," Overton said. "I've got two men down in the jail who *think* you've something of importance to them, and are willing to do you some serious damage because you've got it. I don't know any way you can convince them otherwise, either. They're not the kind of people who do a lot of debating. And they have a gang behind them."

All of a sudden Jeb Lacey felt a weakness in his stomach. He was not a man without courage, but this was not exactly the way things ran in his novels. "But at least you can hold them in the lock-up for a while?"

"Well, you see, that's the problem," Overton said. "As you said a minute or two ago there's no law against smuggling powder—if we can even call it smuggling. And there's no law against paddling a rubber boat in Jamison's Cove either. We can't even hold them for vagrancy. Both have a roll of bills that would choke a horse. So, when we go back to the station this morning, we have to turn them loose. We will, of course, make some suggestions to them about leaving the Commonwealth very rapidly—and they might possibly see their way clear to complying with our suggestion. But then maybe they won't."

"I just don't understand why they went to all that trouble last night," Jeb said. "They could just as easily have driven a car up and parked it over at the library. Instead they go to a lot of trouble to get a boat and sneak it into the cove, and——"

"Just a lousy plot," Overton said sympathetically. "It happens. Just think, how many houses are there at this end of Virginia Street?"

"Just us and the library," Jeb conceded.

"And if they had parked a car out there last night it would be about as conspicuous as a circus elephant. And that we would have noticed, and could have done something about. And now you'll have to excuse us, Mr Lacey. Crime is bustling in Urbanna today."

"And that's it?"

"Not absolutely, no. We'll have somebody in the neighborhood off and on. But I wouldn't advise you to go out too much, at least for a few days. Unless you're planning a world cruise? No?"

"And you don't have any idea *why*?"

"Only one," the detective told him. "From the blankets we found and what you've told us, it has to have been something to do with the baby. You'd best be careful."

"I'll be careful," Jeb told them. "And I have my dog and my shotgun."

"The dog's a fine idea," Overton said, "but be careful of the shotgun. Thieves and mobsters have a lot of rights in court these days. If you shoot one of them they might very well sue you for many, many dollars."

"Yeah, I should be so lucky," Jeb said as he called for Dixon to escort them out. "But at least I'll buy some shells for my shotgun!"

"Rock salt," the detective said as he stepped out onto the porch. "At least they can't sue for as much if you're only shooting rock salt!"

CHAPTER SIX

"IT'S a marvelous day," Meg said as she came into the study, the baby in her arms. "We walked—oh, it seemed like miles." She leaned over and set Eleanor on the floor. The baby immediately started to hump herself across toward Jeb. "And almost every place we went they were decorating for the Oyster Festival."

"I'd almost forgotten," Jeb said.

"Two more weeks," Meg said, the excitement in her voice plain to hear. "Did you know that years ago I was Little Miss Spat?"

"Do you say so? I never did figure out what that was all about."

"And you a Wormeley," Gran Hubbard said disgustedly as she walked into the room, her cane thumping on the floor. Rex had a thing about that cane. At the first thump he got up from his rug and rushed across to the other side of the room.

"Darned dog," Gran muttered. She had done her best to be a friend of every living thing in the house, but Rex was having none of that, and the old lady was hurt. "I left my cat at Mrs Epons' house," she threatened. "Maybe it's time to bring her over here."

Neither Meg nor Jeb answered. Rex growled and huddled in the corner. Gran shrugged and selected the most comfortable chair in the room. "So I'll tell you about Miss Spat." No asking, just a straight shot. Here it is, and you'll listen. Meg *had* always listened, year after year. This time she made a small protest, until Jeb signaled.

"Yes, tell us all about it," he prompted. Gran worked up a satisfied smile. He could almost see the phrase written across her forehead. What a nice young man he is!

"Well, you know that Chesapeake Bay is the world capital of the oyster," the old lady began. "And the Urbanna area is the capital of Virginia's oyster beds. So once a year we have a festival, which includes a grand lot of eating and a parade. The town selects the most beautiful woman around, and she becomes the Oyster Queen."

"And rides a float in the parade," Meg amplified. "I never got to be the Oyster Queen." Jeb shuddered. Oyster Queen? He loved oysters on the half-shell, but—Meg?

Gran sniffed at them both. She hated to have her stories interrupted. "Did you know that a female oyster can lay fifty million eggs in one season? When they hatch but before they begin to make shells they're called spats——"

"If they're hatched," Meg interrupted. Gran Hubbard stared daggers at her. Then Meg suddenly cried, "Look what the baby's doing!"

Every eye turned. Eleanor, having humped her way across the floor, had fallen over on her stomach and begun to crawl on hands and knees toward Rex. Slowly at first, and then with increasing speed and purpose. The old dog, new to the baby trade, sat up and huddled closer to the wall. "She's crawling!" Meg said. "Actually crawling."

"All babies crawl," Gran said. "She's taken a little longer than most."

Meg treated it like a personal insult. "We don't know for sure how old she is, Gran, so we can't judge like that. Anyway, Jeb, the eggs hatch, and it takes five or six years for a shelled oyster to grow to maturity, so in the festival one of the young girls is named Little Miss Spat, and gets to ride on the float with the Oyster Queen, and I was, and that's the whole story."

"Well!" Gran Hubbard struggled to her feet. Jeb went to help. She gave him a smile, and her granddaughter a frown, and stomped out toward the kitchen. "I think I'll give Mrs Brill a little advice."

"And don't be surprised if the dinner is inedible," Meg commented after she had gone. "My gran is a pain in the——."

"Your gran is a little old lady who needs someone to talk to," Jeb interrupted. "Just remember, some day you're liable to be old and gray, just as she is."

"Jeb Lacey, you are impossible."

"Probably."

There was a squeal from the corner. Eleanor, moving faster by the minute, had caught the dog, and didn't know what to do with him. Rex, hoping for the best, sat up and whined. And by that time Jeb was across the room, both hands outstretched. Not for the baby, but for Meg.

She took a startled half-step backward, but was truly trapped. In a second she gave up the struggle and relaxed against him. "What is it?" she asked softly.

"You don't know everything in the world," he told her.

"I know."

"For example, you don't seem to know that I love you."

"You what?"

"I love you. What do you think of that?"

"I—I'm glad to know that, Jeb Lacey."

"And that's all?"

"No, not really. I love you too!"

He sighed in relief. "Thank God for that. You've had me worried for a long time." And then he kissed her. It was not one of his specialty kisses; this one was loaded with comfort, and just the tiniest touch of command.

"Your grandmother needs considerable comforting, Meg. She's slowly recovering from a tough operation, and can't do a lot of the things that she used to do. And now we've isolated her from all her friends, and stuck her in the unenviable position of having an unmarried granddaughter. Just what do you suppose all her church friends will say about that?"

"I know, but it's been a long time, and I can't always keep control of my bad temper, Jeb. The last thing I ever did that won her approval was winning that Little Miss Spat contest. I'm sick of it—and oysters too, by the way!"

His hug was gentle. "But now she's in her eighties, love. Which requires more compassion, more comforting—more listening."

"I—I know that. But I just can't——"

"Yes, you can."

"All right, yes, I can. And Mrs Brill?"

"I've already had a word with Dixon about it. He'll take care of the rest of the staff. That's what butlers do."

"All right. I'll do better. If you'll do better."

"I thought I was doing pretty well with Gran."

"Oh, you are. Sometimes you're doing so well it turns my stomach. No, I don't mean with Gran, I mean with me. That last kiss was what I would rate as a brother-in-law kiss."

"Aha!" And he proceeded to rectify his error.

When he was done with her—her thought, not his—he collapsed into his computer chair, breathing heavily. She stood flat-footed in front of him and laughed. True, her face was flushed blood-red, her hair was a mass of confusion, her eyes gleamed like those of a feral hunter, and the whole weight of her rocked back and forth. But she was still able to stand up, and he couldn't.

"It's not polite to laugh," he complained. "A man has some pride, after all."

"Do I presume from all this that we're engaged?" she asked prettily.

"You do," he muttered, and began to comb through his desk and his pockets looking for something. "Ah! Here! Hold out your hand."

"Which one?"

"I don't know," he said. "You can't expect me to know everything in the world, can you?"

So she offered him her left hand, and struggled to hold down the giggling as he tried to flip open a small jeweler's box with one hand while holding her arm with the other. But when he managed to get the box open all thoughts of giggling vanished. The ring was plain and simple, a platinum band supporting a massive diamond, itself surrounded by a glow of emerald chips, all glowing in the sun.

"Is this where I say, Oh, you shouldn't have?" she asked.

"Don't be coy," he muttered. "Put the damn thing on. Is that the right finger?"

"I believe so," she said. "In America, that is. I understand in some parts of France it goes on the other hand." She held her left hand up to catch the glitter. It seemed almost like a small star. "And you really shouldn't have, Jeb. Something much smaller would have served the purpose."

"I wasn't interested in serving the purpose," he said as he pulled her closer and tighter. "I was interested in advertising to all the world that you're taken!"

"I don't know but that a slave-auction might have served better," she said, smiling up at him with misty eyes. "Should I expect that you'll make one of those dominant husbands?"

"You'd better believe it," he muttered as he pulled her down onto his lap and kissed her again.

Ha! she thought. Have you got a lot to learn, Mr Lacey! And I'm going to be the teacher! She looked over at the dog. Rex was still sitting up, with head held high— out of reach, so to speak. Eleanor had scrambled up to him, turned around, and now sat between his forelegs, the dog's chin just resting on top of the baby's head. Both were grinning. As was Jeb.

"Smart alecs," she muttered, and weaseled her way out of Jeb's arms, just as Gran Hubbard came back into the room, this time riding her wheelchair.

"Yes, you're right," Annie Mae said. "The house is jammed with smart alecs. That woman has got to go!"

"Our cook?" Meg and Jeb both exclaimed at the same time.

"So-called cook," Annie Mae said. "Why didn't you tell me she came from Tappahannock? She doesn't know beans about cooking oysters! And just what were the police doing here this morning?"

Dixon came hurrying in behind her, in shirtsleeves. "I'm sorry," he said. "It slipped out. Gertrude. I'll see that it doesn't happen again."

"And why," Annie Mae continued, "do we have to have this great big hulking man in the house? Butler? Ha!"

"I don't understand the complaint, Annie Mae," Jeb said. "Butlers have to carry heavy things, and move stuff. Yourself, for example. If it hadn't been for Dixon we would never have gotten you into the house when we brought you back from the hospital. Remember?"

"Hmmph!" Gran Hubbard said. "Well—I didn't remember that. And about the police? Gives a house a bad name, police running in and out all over the place."

"Nothing to that, Gran. It's the police benefit. I agreed to buy a dozen tickets. For the police widows and orphans, you'll remember."

Annie Mae looked puzzled. "It must be my memory. I don't remember that either. I think I'd better take a nap before dinner. Dixon?" The suddenly weakened lady gestured, and Dixon took the handles of the wheelchair and pushed her back to her bedroom. Mrs Brill poked her head around the doorjamb after they had gone.

"Am I fired?"

"Not a chance," Jeb said. "Not a chance. Little old ladies, you know."

"I know," the cook said. "I've worked in a mess of houses with little old ladies in them."

"And while you're at it," Meg said firmly, "what *were* the police doing here? And if you don't mind I'd like you to stare me in the eye. You are the smoothest—man I've ever met."

"*Look* you straight in the eye," he promised, and then winked at her as he told her all about it. Well, as much about it as he thought he might get away with.

"And so we don't know anything more about anything than we did before?" Her eyes were glued on him; no chance to escape.

"Hardly anything. Except there's something going on about the baby, and it would appear that a Mafia gang has something to do with it all, and we'd better be more careful than we have been. Hence Dixon."

"Hence Dixon? What does he have to do with us and the baby?"

"Surely you've noticed, dear, what a very large man Dixon is?"

"Oh, for heaven's sakes. A bodyguard?"

"Well, at least we could say a *babyguard*."

"I—I——" she stuttered. "If I didn't love you so much I'd pack up and head for the back country."

"Good idea," he said. "Take me with you."

Annie Mae came out for dinner, full of vim and vigor. Jeb looked at Meg.

"I showed her my ring," Meg whispered. "She approves. Although she did say we—she and I—had to go back to her house for a day, tomorrow, because the garden club is coming, and she needs me to——"

"Serve?" Jeb asked. Meg shook her head.

"Show," she corrected as she waved her ringed hand just under the edge of the table. "You wouldn't mind?"

"Me? Obviously I don't have a thing to do with it. I've done my part. Now all I have to do is say, Yes, ma'am, and things of that nature."

"You'd better not stop writing," she threatened. "Have some oysters?"

"Surely not every night?" he pleaded.

"Eat," she coaxed. "I understand it's a great aphrodisiac."

"Do you really?" he asked in a roundly disgusted voice. "And what good would that do me, the way things are around this place?"

"Well, who knows?" she murmured. "You could get lucky."

"Pass the oysters," Jeb Lacey said. Annie Mae smiled widely.

"That's a good boy," she said, pushing the deep dish of oyster fritters in his direction. Meg Hubbard snickered, and then ducked her head into her napkin. *Good*, she knew, was not the sort of *boy* he hoped to be.

Annie Mae Hubbard went to bed later than usual, happier than usual. That huge sparkler on her granddaughter's finger had erased practically all of her doubts and suspicions. Once tucked in, Gran spent three quarters of an hour building and rebuilding scenarios for the morrow's meeting of the garden club. And while Meg listened Jeb played with the baby, bathed her, dressed her for her evening's sleep, and pondered a new plot, one having to do with a kidnapped baby and an errant mother.

So when Meg came from one victory—over her grandmother—and snatched up the baby for her second victim, Jeb felt just the slightest bit put out. It wasn't enough to fall in love with Meg; he was equally taken with young Eleanor Whatever-her-last-name-might-be. His word processor responded to his fingers.

First a tentative scattering of words, and then a full flow, high speed. *The Baby Caper*, he titled it. A full-blown mystery, redolent of mayhem—and two murders tucked in for his agent's sake. Saul loved murders, as long as all the blood was off-stage.

Gradually the house slowed down around him; Virginia Street traffic faded away. Meg and Eleanor had disappeared upstairs. Dixon had checked the locks and disappeared into his third-floor bedroom. Gertrude had gone home to Cross Street, and Mrs Brill had been picked up by her husband. Head down, fingers properly positioned to avoid the strain, Jeb Lacey pecked away at a hundred words a minute and the story unfolded.

It was the silence that disturbed him. Everything had ceased. Wind and weather and sirens and auto noises, all gone. He lifted his fingers off the keyboard, pushed his chair back, and stood up, and stretched. The back of his neck was stiff, a sure sign that a great deal of time had passed. The kitchen clock struck. Three o'clock? Disbelieving, he walked out into the kitchen. The chimes on the old clock agreed with the hands. Three o'clock. He took a quick peek into Gran Hubbard's room. The old lady was rolled up into a ball, fast asleep.

I've forgotten something, he told himself. What? Three in the morning, a Hubbard rolled up in a ball, fast asleep. "You could get lucky." Meg! "When bigger idiots are born, they'll all be Laceys," he muttered. A quick dash into the bathroom to brush his teeth and rinse. No need for washing; it would be solid darkness upstairs. A gentle brushing of hair, and a little squeamish feeling. Jeb Lacey, you are thirty-four years old and your hair is not what it used to be! He dashed for the stairs.

All this movement had awakened Rex. The old dog, Mr Curiosity himself, wandered over to the stairs just at the moment that Jeb stretched out a foot toward the first riser. Collision was inevitable.

"Damn dog," Jeb snarled as he got up off his bruised posterior. Rex, who ought to have known enough to get out of the way but didn't, moved closer and licked his face. "Not now!" Jeb pushed him away, scrambled to his feet, and raced up the stairs, minus one slipper.

The night-light was on in the baby's room, but Meg was not there. Her bed had not been turned down. A shot of excitement raced up Jeb's spine. "Where are you, love?" he muttered as he backed out into the corridor. It had been a long time between—drinks, so to speak.

There was a vague glow of light shining in his window, from the single streetlight out on Virginia Street. Just enough light to make out that there was a lump in his bed. The little nursery story pummeled his brain. "'And somebody's sleeping in my bed,' said the baby bear!"

Cautiously he approached the bed. Meg Hubbard, dressed tastefully in nothing at all, scrooched over to the far side of the bed, smiling in her sleep. Only the sheet covered her, and that only from the knees down. Her magnificent golden hair was spread over the adjacent pillow.

Jeb Lacey drew in a deep sharp breath. It had been years since he had gone regularly to church. "A 'Home' Baptist", his grandmother used to call him. But here was the proper time for a thank-you prayer. So he made it, before he stepped out of his clothes and carefully sidled into the empty side of the bed. Meg stirred not an inch. Just looking at her in the semi-darkness, the gold of her hair, the caress that was her smile, the soft full curve of her breasts—all were just enough to fire up his engine. He edged over to his bedside table and pulled out the necessary protection.

"Now then, love," he whispered as he moved, flat on his back, almost up to her side. And Meg moved as well. She rolled over on her side, facing him, and rested her head and shoulder on *his* shoulder. Her weight fastened his shoulder to the bed. He rocked gently back and forth a time or two, with no result. So try another try, he told himself.

Turned on her side, not only did Meg's head rest on his shoulder, but her right breast nibbled at his nipple. His other hand came over her chest and cupped her left breast. He squeezed gently, caressed, stroked. Meg made a troubled move, and then returned to the original position.

Try again, he told himself. His hand moved again, toying with her taut nipple. She moaned and squirmed uneasily, pinning his legs to the mattress by crossing over him with one of her own long, shapely legs. And then she lay still. He moved a little closer.

There has to be a way, Jeb thought. How do you turn on a woman who is fast asleep? Yell in her ear? No, that certainly didn't seem the way to do things. But— she has more sensitive areas than those lovely swollen breasts. He grinned to himself and let his hand run down her breast onto her stomach, down to the mound of Venus, and off into space. He knew the place; experience was a great teacher. That one tiny little spot— and his finger found it and pressed.

Meg Hubbard came awake with a start. She started to sit up, only to find her long hair trapped beneath his muscular frame. And it hurt. "Ouch! What the devil are you trying to do to me?" she roared. "Scalp me?"

Rex pattered up the stairs; the baby woke up and started to cry. Jeb bounced over in the bed, and landed on the floor. Meg came to the edge of the bed and peered down at him.

"Well?" she said coldly.

"If I told you you wouldn't believe," he said morosely. "You couldn't believe."

"So the baby's crying and you're the closest. Why don't you show me what a good fellow you are and see what she needs?"

"Yeah. Baby," he muttered as he struggled to his feet and fumbled around for his robe. "Good boy," he grumbled as he headed for the door.

"Good boy?" Meg recalled the phrase at dinner. "Is that what this is all about? You wanted to——?"

"Aw, shut up," Jeb snapped as he went into the baby's room.

Baby Eleanor was really upset. He changed her, produced the stand-by bottle of formula, walked the floor with her, sang little snatches of songs that he almost remembered, rocked her in the rocking chair, and finally coaxed Rex to come and put his cool nose on her stomach. And at that, at nearly four in the morning, little Eleanor chortled and went to sleep. The blankets in the child's crib were as wet as her diapers had been. Holding the baby with one hand, Jeb managed to strip and change every little thing, until finally, with care and affection, he managed to get her down in her crib, still sleeping.

"Thank you, dog," he muttered sarcastically as he backed out of the baby's room, and then wheeled around without a sound and headed back into his own bedroom.

"Eleanor's asleep again," he whispered as he came over to the side of his own still occupied bed. And then he sealed his lips and cursed up a silent storm—because so was Meg Hubbard!

One of the things Jeb Lacey had learned during his brief education in the military was how to leave a trail of silent curses behind him . . . all the way downstairs to the wine closet, through two glasses of cognac, and back to his computer chair.

"Now how in the whole world did that happen?" he asked the walls, the clock, the dog, the computer. And got no answer. So back he went to his latest novel, grinding into it everything he could remember from the lovable night just past. "Who knows?" Meg had said. "You might get lucky."

He had had a whole bucketful of luck in just one night. All bad! And by the time he had added another chapter to his latest story there was sunlight peering into his study window, the kitchen clock struck seven, and Mrs Brill arrived to make breakfast.

"Going to be a fine day," the cook said as she brought him in his mug of tea. "Up late again, Mr Lacey? Seems as though writing books is a tough darn business. I told my husband about it, and he said it ain't just worth it, all the work for such small pay."

"Yes, but if that's all I can do, book-writing just has to be it. What is it your husband does?"

"He's a tonger. You know, digs oysters with a pair of tongs?"

"Now that must bring in a fine lot of money," Jeb said. "Almost as much as a policeman?"

"More than that," Mrs Brill said. "But of course, bein' a policeman, you're on the city and don't get no seasonal layoffs. Ham and eggs this morning? Or would you rather have oysters?"

"Would you believe," Jeb told her, sighing, "I think I might be allergic to oysters?"

"Poor man," Mrs Brill said. "I'll slice the ham. And Mrs Hubbard is stirring already, did you know?"

"She gets priority," Jeb told her. "There's a meeting of the garden club this morning."

Mrs Brill shook her head. She didn't approve of clubs for women. Or rather, her husband didn't approve of clubs for women, and didn't hesitate to let everyone know. Strange life, Mrs Brill told herself. Poor Mrs Lacey's man's doin' the only thing he knows to do—sits here all day and all night and writes books.

Those books with the fancy covers on them, too. I'm thinkin' to read one of them any one of these days—if I can hide it from Harold, who would certainly not approve! Maybe I could get one from the bookstore with a plain brown wrapper on it?

And so, clutching her little secret to her bosom like a prospective bank robber, she went back to preparing Gran Hubbard's breakfast.

Meg and the baby came downstairs a few minutes later. Eleanor was all gurgles and laughter. Meg was solemn-eyed, with a worry-line in her forehead. She sat the baby down in her playpen and moved hesitantly toward Jeb.

"I'm sorry," she said cautiously.

"No reason to be."

"Yes, but I—I was so tired I just couldn't keep awake. What took you so long?"

"I was stricken by a sudden attack of stupidity," Jeb remarked. "It just struck me why women in the old days wore nightcaps when they went to bed."

Meg gently patted the top of her head. "I really thought you were trying to scalp me," she said. Her lower lip was trembling, and something was glistening in her right eye. "I don't know a lot about this—business, Jeb. I haven't—well, I haven't—not yet, anyway—and I think I might have—did you?"

"Don't tell me—at your age? A virgin?"

"So it isn't funny," she fumed at him. "If I see one little laugh I'm going to give you such a knock. Well, did you?"

"If it's any help to your morale, no, I didn't. It wasn't for want of trying, but I didn't."

"But I thought—you—all that experience. All those books..."

"It didn't help. Not a bit."

"Then I'm—sorry. I knew you wanted to, and I'd worked up enough courage to let it happen, but I didn't count on falling asleep in the middle of things."

"Neither did I," he groaned, and then studied her face. It wasn't *her* fault, not by any means. He shrugged and mustered up a reasonably good smile. "Let's drop the subject. You have a busy day ahead of you."

"And you can take care of Eleanor while I'm gone?"

"I suppose I might be able to."

But, whatever the plan, it flew apart when Annie Mae, all perfumed and powdered and wearing her best dress, bounced into the study. "What? The baby's not dressed?"

"I thought to leave her in her nappy," Jeb said. "It's showing signs of a hot day, and she'll be more comfortable that way."

"Men! You just don't understand. Eleanor is going with us, of course. Everybody will want to know, and she's such a cute little thing."

"Looks like a Hubbard," Jeb teased. Gran turned four shades of red, sputtering, unable to get a word out. Until finally she took a deep breath.

"My doctor," she said, "told me to keep calm. So look at me, I'm keeping calm. But if I had my umbrella here, young man, I'd show you a thing or two. Looks like a Hubbard, indeed!"

"Well, she sure as the devil doesn't look like a Lacey," Jeb averred. "It's that olive skin of hers. She looks more like an Italian than a Lacey, and Meg told me that there's Italian blood in her family line.''

"I," Annie Mae announced, "am going back to my room for five minutes. And when I come back I want to see Meg and the baby dressed, and I don't ever want to hear again about Italian blood. Is that clear?"

Jeb watched, mouth half-open, as the little old lady stamped out. "What did I say now?" he asked Meg plaintively. She was busy dressing Eleanor as best she could.

"A slight family feud," she told him over her shoulder. "The Hubbards and the D'Agostinos felt that each of them got the bad side of the marriage when my grandfather married Sophia. The only times they get together are for weddings and funerals. I'll tell you about it some day."

"I don't know that I want to hear," Jeb said. "Are you taking the Cadillac?"

"I can't drive that thing," Meg said. "It's like driving a tank uphill through the mud."

"So that," he explained, "is why we hired Dixon. He drives."

"And he also butles?"

"As you say. And he also packs a pair of brass knuckles. Hates to skin his knuckles, he told me."

"Where did you—how did you get to know these people, Jeb? Dixon, Mrs Brill?"

"In the war, love. Dixon was my first soldier. Mr Brill was in charge of our nighttime food supplies."

"In charge of——?"

"Our nighttime food supplies. Surely you knew that the army never quite gets necessary things distributed on time? Sergeant Brill was in charge of equalizing the distribution. He worked nights, mostly."

"You mean he *stole* food?"

"That's not quite the right word. Listen. The food was maintained at quartermaster supply points. Naturally the quartermaster people couldn't eat all that, and they worked so hard they went to bed early. So Brill merely took our share just a little bit ahead of time. Don't bother your head with it; it's very complicated— not the sort of thing to bother your pretty head about." He looked out the window. "There's the car now. You'd better get a bustle on, before your gran chews you up into little pieces. Who's going with you?"

"Just Gran and I. And the baby. And Gertrude to take care of the baby. And Dixon."

"And you're leaving Mrs Brill to take care of my needs? How nice."

"Not exactly."

He started to come up out of his chair. She planted a dainty hand in the middle of his chest and pushed him back down. "You needn't worry. Mrs Brill has gone on ahead to prepare the goodies for the party. But she made a bunch of sandwiches for you before she left in case you get hungry. The refrigerator is stacked full. You'll enjoy!"

"Not oyster sandwiches?"

Meg's face turned two shades of pale white as she snatched up the baby and headed for the front door.

"You'll be sorry for this," Jeb roared after her.

She waved at him over her shoulder. "Jeb, there's a man here to see you." And with that she was gone.

Jeb got up and wandered toward the front door. He was still in his pajamas, unshaven—nor finished his breakfast, for that matter. And there *was* a man at the door. A short and very rotund man dressed in a fine blue-striped three-piece suit, a necktie of various shades of pink and yellow, a pair of black and white shoes, and sporting a supersized cigar. Unlit. He looked to be five feet six in all directions.

"Lacey?" he asked in a raspy deep voice.

"Yes?"

"Fangold. I unnerstan' you recently—acquired a little baby boy?"

"I'm afraid not, Mr——?"

"Call me Frank. Big Frank."

"Well, Frank, somebody told you an untruth. We have recently acquired a little baby girl. In the usual manner, of course."

"A girl?"

"A girl."

"You wouldn't lie to me?"

"No reason why I should."

"It could be dangerous if you did," Frank Fangold said. "Dangerous. Hell, you don't even know who I am, do you? I'd like to see this kid."

"I'm afraid that's not possible. My—er—wife has taken her over to the garden club. Your name—you're Italian, I suppose?"

"Right. What's that got to do with anything?"

"Nothing, really. It's just that my wife has Italian blood in her family. The D'Agostinos, you know."

"Nice name," the little man commented. He visibly relaxed. "But I still gotta see this baby."

"So come back later," Jeb suggested. "Come for lunch. We often have oysters."

"Oysters?"

"A great aphrodisiac," Jeb said solemnly.

The man's eyes flared. Look at that, Jeb told himself. A true believer!

"So I'll come," Big Frank said. "Maybe today. I ain't sure." And off he went down the drive, where a gray stretch limousine waited for him. Jeb stood at the door, still half opened, wondering what other kind of character he might pick up for his next book. Only after the limo had pulled out into Virginia Street did he close the door behind him and head for the refrigerator.

CHAPTER SEVEN

"SO, IN spite of your lack of feelings for the Little Old Ladies' Club, you had a good time?" Jeb was lying flat on the floor, bouncing the baby on his chest. Eleanor treated it all as a great treat, chortling as she bounced. And Jeb was going out of his way to hide the fact that up until a few minutes before they arrived home he had been napping on the couch.

Meg grinned at him. "What's this, the 'I told you so' review?"

He grinned back at her. "Everyone's entitled, love."

"I like the way you say that—'love'. Yes, I had a grand time of it. The house was packed. There must have been thirty or thirty-five members of the club there. They oohed and ahed at the baby, but they saved their best remarks for the ring. I waved my hand around like one of the Anointed, and Gran wouldn't even let me wash the dishes. I haven't been so royally treated since I won the Spat award. And let me tell you that was a long time ago!"

"Well, lucky you. Nothing else worth reporting?"

"There were four or five of them who did their best to crowd me into a corner and ask me to explain just exactly how we acquired this—child."

"And you told them?"

"That it was your sister's baby, and we were just taking care of it for her while she went to Toronto."

"But in every good plot there must be an explanation. What is she doing in Toronto?"

118

"Well, that's where the hush-hush comes into play. Toronto is famous for its medical facilities, you know."

"No, I didn't know that."

"Well, it is. I know because I say it is, and since I'm the author of this plot you have to accept it as gospel truth. Actually, the big medical center is in Montreal, but I don't speak French, and neither does the baby, so I couldn't very well say——"

He waved a hand at her. "Of course. And, as you say, it's your plot, to do whatever you want to with. But keep me posted.

"I had a visitor while you were out. A gentleman by the name of Fangold. Big Frank Fangold. Sound familiar?"

"Not a bit. Just because one of my grandmothers was Italian it doesn't mean that I know all the people in the world with Italian-sounding names. Maybe he wasn't even Italian. There are a lot of Italians with red hair and blue eyes. What did he want?"

"Thank you very much for the lecture. I know some Italians who are blonds, too. And I once had an editor with an Italian-sounding name whose family came to England with the Norman invaders. How about that? Anyway, this man had a perfectly fine New York accent. And he wanted to talk to me about the boy-child we had recently acquired. He was much discouraged to hear it was a girl. So much so that he said he had to be sure it wasn't a boy, and he would come around one day and inspect. So I invited him for lunch. How about that?"

"I have no idea how about that," she said, sighing. "Jeb Lacey, you are the most careless man with the truth that I've ever known."

"I don't write fact," he returned. "I write fiction."

"Did you know," she mused, "that up until I met you I never, ever told a lie? Well, hardly ever. And now they're rolling off my tongue like cars on the assembly line. Lucky I'm not a Catholic—I'd have to spend hours in the confessional—days, maybe!"

"You mean there aren't any confessions in your church?"

"Well, we have a general confession, but it's not—you didn't say how you enjoyed your sandwiches."

"No, I didn't, did I?" The moment of silence seemed to run for hours.

"And you're not going to? Gran spent a lot of time manufacturing those."

"Well, hooray for Gran. That's the first time I've ever been face to face with oyster sandwiches. That may well be the last time I eat oysters. Did I ever tell you that it's possible I'm allergic to oysters? I've already warned Mrs Brill. Even Rex wouldn't touch those sandwiches. He might be allergic too."

Meg's face fell. She brushed her hair back off her face and stared at him. "You're making that up. People aren't allergic to oysters—I think. And dogs are absolutely never allergic to oysters. That's an absolute truth. You know that if you were allergic to oysters you would have to leave the Chesapeake? And maybe it's even unpatriotic. You mean you didn't eat *anything*?"

"That's about it. Good for the waistline, bad for the stomach."

"Oh, Jeb! Let me fix you something—no oysters, I promise."

"I don't have time," he said. "I'm planning a research trip out to St George's School. Right away. Ten minutes ago, for a fact."

"St George's? That's a boys' school. What in the world are you up to now?"

"Research," he said casually. "That's how I make my living. I write books. Every book has to be in some specific place. So I do research. That's what you're doing on your magazine article, isn't it?"

"Then Eleanor and I are coming with you."

"Insistent little thing, aren't you? Of course you're both coming."

"Don't give me that 'little' bit. I'm big enough. And I'll make you a ham sandwich to take with us."

"If you insist. But get a little speed on. I have an appointment with the headmaster in fifty-five minutes."

He drove the Cadillac himself. Dixon had caught a case of sniffles, and remained behind with a set of instructions big enough to choke a horse.

"And not to worry about little foreigners," the big man promised.

"You'd better worry," Jeb said. "He's the type of little fellow who will pull out a gun and shoot you dead if he's a mind to."

So, after many assurances of care, they went off to the countryside. Not very far into the countryside, for a fact. St George's was a private school with a grouping of attractive brick and stone buildings, a delightful playing field and a curving paved road almost surrounding it.

"For resident boys from nine to twelve," the headmaster told him when they settled in his office.

"And some day-boys and girls of the same age. Now, the name of your young person is——?"

"Eleanor," Meg interrupted. The man smiled.

"Ah. A girl. And just when will she be nine?"

"You understand, Dr Winston, we would like to see the school and its facilities before we take steps?"

"Of course, of course. What could I have been thinking of? Let me call a reliable member of our senior class to show you around. No interference from biased staff members, eh? What did you say you did for a living, Mr Lacey?"

"I write novels," Jeb said, and reeled off six or seven names under which he was presently writing. The head was suitably impressed. He had actually read two or three of Jeb's travel books. There was not a mention of murders or romances or adventures. I wonder why? Meg asked herself, and laughed at her own joke. Both the men looked up at her curiously, and little Eleanor, who had been sleeping in a carry-basket beside Meg's chair, opened one eye as if to ask, What has Mommy done now?

A long fifty minutes later they were back in the headmaster's office. Jeb had run off two rolls of color snapshots, and used up two rolls of eight-millimeter tape in his camcorder, and then packed it all away. Their guide, who was a well-qualified young man, and a star on the school's football team—soccer that was—had worn himself down to a frazzle, toting little Eleanor in her basket.

"And that," Jeb told Meg as he stuffed exposed film into his carryall, "should be enough material to make one, maybe two novels."

"Jeb Lacey! Is that what we really came for?"

"Of course. Surely you don't think that everything in my books comes out of my imagination? Now, one last session with the boss, and we're off."

"So you've decided," the headmaster said. He was obviously tired. It was near the end of the school day.

And everyone who had ever dealt with the demands of a school day filled by nine-year-old boys would realize how tired he might be.

"Yes," Jeb said. "I think we've decided. We would like to reserve a space for Eleanor."

"Excellent, Mr—er—Lacey." He asked a dozen questions, filling out a form before him on the desk. But it was not until he heard the answer to the last question that the smile faded. "Now, when will little Eleanor be nine years old?"

Jeb was struck with a coughing fit. Meg, having proved her worth at the garden club, stepped into the breach. "Eight years, two months and six days," she said sweetly. "And I'm sure she'll be an apt pupil!"

"You're serious?" Now it was the headmaster's time for coughing.

"Well, you do mention advanced reservations in your brochure," Jeb said. "And we know how crowded schools of your calibre can get—so we thought, Why not now?"

The headmaster was a man of many parts. "And why not now?" he agreed as he finished filling out the papers.

Outside in the parking lot Meg took the baby out of the confining basket and waited for a moment while Jeb started the engine and turned on the air-conditioning. It was a warm day for so late in the autumn season, and the leather seats were too hot for comfort. She leaned against the open door while dandling the baby. "Now, perhaps you could tell what that was all about?"

"What? The visit?"

"Yes, the visit. Notice, Jeb, how cautious I've become. Whatever it was that we did, why?"

"A number of things," he said quietly. "First of all, it's a fine school, and I wanted to settle Eleanor into a reserved spot."

"Yeah, I'll bet. Eight years ahead of time you're reserving her a seat as a day student? Pull my other leg, love."

"Sceptical, lady? But nice legs, believe me. If pulling one of them represents an advance in our relationship, I'd be——"

"Don't do that," she squeaked. "I'll drop the baby! Don't do that, you darn—lecher!"

"OK, lady, but just remember you invited me. Maybe tonight. That would be nice."

And maybe it would, Meg thought. We'll go home and I'll get a nap and then we'll see. Won't we?

But he wasn't going back out to the highway. He drove around the semicircle of the playing fields, to where a small chapel of ancient design stood almost alone among the trees.

"Christ Church. I want to visit with my ancestors," he said. "All the early ones are buried out in back of the chapel here."

"I'm not at all convinced why we came out here," she repeated. "A little better explanation would be nice. It certainly wasn't all about Eleanor."

The road was narrow. He maneuvered the big Cadillac off onto the grass by the side of the chapel, cut the motor, and turned in her direction. "And that's where you're wrong," he said quietly. "It *was* all about Eleanor. Don't you remember I told you about Big Frank Fangold?"

"Big Frank? He sounds like a Mafia don. And if Eleanor had been a boy Frank would have done something drastic, I'll bet. Something like taking her away from us. He *did* sound like Mafia."

"I suppose he is," Jeb told her. "Only I didn't find out until this morning. I had a talk with Lieutenant Overton. Big Frank is some kind of capo in the New York mob. And like a bright boy I invited him to come to lunch today. After I found out what he was I decided that a nice visit in the country would be a fine thing for all three of us. Come on, girls, we're really going to stroll among my ancestors."

He climbed out of the car and came around to relieve her of the child. The baby gave a crow of delight and nestled against his shoulder. "Man-crazy," Meg said, and then, under her breath, "Me too!"

"I do believe you're jealous," he returned. "Watch where you're walking. There are all kinds of things to fall over. I should have asked you to leave your high heels at home."

Jealous? she thought. You'd better believe it, buster. And I don't know why. I'm jealous of everything and everybody who gets close to you. Even my gran! Is this some sort of mania—or some sort of love? Will I do better if we get married? When we get married. Will we get married?

"Watch it," he said. She took his arm, and little Eleanor squealed. See, it's him, Meg told herself. Even the baby is jealous.

"Don't step there," Jeb said. "That's where the second Ralph Wormeley is buried." Meg looked down at the low stone crypt, worn with age and weather.

"How in the world can you tell?" she asked. "You certainly can't read any of that inscription."

"I don't have to," he said, chuckling. "My great-grandmother told me. But hey, it's almost four o'clock. Let's scoot out of here. I'm sure the coast is clear back in Urbanna."

"You'd better not be wrong," she threatened as she hugged both of them. "You owe me a kiss, Mr Lacey."

He offered to repay his debt, from wherever he had accumulated it. It was a nice lively kiss, but unfortunately the school field hockey team, which had been practicing behind them, came by and made a few remarks. Nothing substantial, of course. None of them was over twelve. But Meg was still somewhat shy.

She fled back to the car, with Jeb and the baby following along, exchanging remarks with the boys. And then home. Eleanor was happy all the way. There seemed to be something about the hum of the tires, the smooth thrust of the motor that calmed the little girl and, finally, coaxed her to sleep.

By about eight o'clock Jeb was sitting in the study, on the old divan which he had resurrected some days earlier. Dressed in pajamas and a light robe, he had one foot up on a leather hassock, while the other was rocking the cradle in which Eleanor was happily asleep. Meg came in quietly from her gran's rooms, where she had been serving as a sounding board for Annie Mae's memories.

"You look tired," she said as she squeezed in beside him on the divan. His arm automatically came around her.

"I am—worn to the bone, and I don't know why."

She squirmed around to face him, and ran one of her hands through his hair. "You've been busier than a one-armed paper-hanger," she said. "You need rest."

"Sure, but I can get plenty of that after I've gone. Visiting that cemetery this afternoon marked me up a little bit. All my ancestors. Well, not *all* of them. There's a bunch of them scattered from here to Memphis, Tennessee as well."

"You really *are* in the doldrums." She pulled her feet up under her, leaned over, and gently kissed his cheek. "I knew something was wrong when I looked in and you weren't at the word processor."

"Oh? And what have you been up to?"

"I helped Mrs Brill clean up the kitchen, and then I sat and listened to Gran until it was her bedtime. She wanted to talk about how things were when she was a little girl. Lord, what a wild bunch of memories. Do you know what Gran and her boy friends used to do in the rumble seat of her dad's old car?"

"I don't think I want to know," he said gently. "I'm not even sure what a rumble seat is. Something to do with cars?" He ran his hand through her lush weight of golden hair. "You know, we shouldn't try to steal *her* memories. After all, we'll have some of our own one of these days."

"I wasn't stealing hers," Meg snapped. "I was sharing them. There's a difference."

"And that's a part of my problem too," he admitted. "I've come across the biggest writer's block I've ever seen. The story is not only not going well, it's not going at all."

"*The Baby Caper*?" she asked.

"*The Baby Caper*. I've got the model right there in front of me, but I can't get her down on paper." He gestured down toward little Eleanor. "My problem is that I'm not sure how things are going to turn out for this little lady in real life. I'd love to get my hands on that sister of mine and pull her into little pieces. Ordinarily, in all my books I know where I'm going—not this time, I don't. And I'm not the bravest man you ever met, love. So I've got this funny little feeling in the pit of my stomach and it just won't go away."

"That man is causing all this turmoil? Big Frank?"

"Yes, isn't that a laugher? Five feet six, two hundred fifty pounds? Big Frank?"

"I wish I could help, but I've run up against a block on my magazine article myself. Funny thing. I've got a rip-roaring story from the day you were born until you graduated from high school. My editor keeps telephoning twice a day. And..."

"You've run out of material?"

"No, Lord, no. I've got enough material to write a complete biography, but every time I sit down to work I discover..."

"Discover what? Spit it out."

Meg took a deep breath, as if preparing to make a dive into a shallow swimming pool. "I discover that I don't want to tell all those nosy people the wonderful things I know about you. I want to keep you to myself!"

He grinned down at her. She was as neat as a pin, her hair all braided, her blouse buttoned to the top, her skirts folded neatly around her. And yet she had that gamine look that he loved.

"The trouble with you, woman, is that you've got your head on too tight." One of his hands tugged at the pins that held her braids up in a tight circle around her brow. The braid fell away, and he fumbled for the band that held it all together. She reached up to stop him.

"Remember what happened the last time you and my hair came to blows," she said.

"Yes, but I didn't know all the rules that time," he teased. "Maybe we could have a re-match some time soon."

"I wouldn't be against it," she said, sighing. "A girl can't be a virgin forever."

"What a nice thought. Next week is the first weekend in November. That would be—Friday and Saturday, or something like that."

"And?"

"That would be the weekend of the Oyster Festival."

"Yes?"

"I just happened to be talking to the Reverend Stanton."

"A very nice man." It won her another hug. "His church is only about two blocks away from Gran's house," she told him.

"Yes, we spoke about your gran."

"And that's it? You had nothing else to say?" Stop stalling, Jeb Lacey, Meg told herself. Get to the point, if there is one. If we ever get married I'll need a buggy whip to make you get to the point! If we ever get married? A tiny tear formed in the corner of her left eye. *If!*

"Oh, no, we had lots of other things to say. He asked about you and whether you were ever coming back to the congregation."

"And you said..."

"Very soon, I told him. And then he——"

"Very soon?"

"Hush, woman." One of his fingers came up and gently tapped her nose. She shook her head and sighed. If he wasn't going to tell her, he just wasn't going to. She had learned enough about him to know little things like that.

"So the parson said he had this little problem."

Meg sat up straight and watched. He *was* going to tell her. In his own long-drawn-out manner, of course, but he was going to...

"He said that every year during the festival the Wesleyan ladies of his church make and sell oyster stew."

Meg slumped again. "Everybody knows that," she grumbled. "It's good. The stew, that is. Gran uses her recipe—my other grandmother's—the Italian lady."

"But what they need," Jeb continued, "is some sort of attraction to increase the glamor of the affair. So I made him a suggestion."

Meg sat up again, furious at him. "Stop beating around the bush," she demanded as she beat on his shoulder with her little fist. "You suggested what?"

"Well, what are churches for?" he said, moving to trap her hand before she broke it or his shoulder. "Weddings, of course. I suggest that he ought to find the right young couple and put on a wedding."

"A—make-believe wedding?"

"No, love, that wouldn't do. A *real* wedding. You and me—or is it you and I?"

"I don't know," she gasped. "You're the writer. I like you and me better. A real wedding? Do you mean it?"

"I'd better," he said, chuckling. "I also got the license, had the Reverend post the banns, ordered a new flower-girl's dress for Eleanor, and—are you ready for this?—called my mother!"

"Your mother's going to come?"

"I don't know about that. It's the racing season in Paris. But who knows? She might."

"I'm not—sure—that I'm prepared for that much," Meg said. "I've heard around town that your mother is some kind of..."

"Dragon," Jeb filled in. "But you needn't worry. Just as long as I haven't signed her check she'll behave herself."

"And your sister?"

His smile fled. "I wish I knew where the hell she is," he said. "My sister is a strange fish—but she's still my sister. I think a lot of her. I've hired a detective agency to look for her, by the way."

"That's nice, but if she comes she might take the baby away from us," Meg said dolefully.

"Good lord, I never thought of that," he said. "Well, that's just one more river to cross. Oh, I forgot. There's one little item left. And this time it's for real. Will you marry me, Meg?"

Meg Hubbard gave a little squeal and threw both hands around his neck. "You just try to get away from me," she gloated.

He swept her up in his arms, managing to kick the baby's cradle in the doing. Eleanor awoke with a terrible temper tantrum, and just then the doorbell rang.

The pair of them froze in position. "All the staff have gone?" he asked.

"All," she said. "Dixon was the last to leave. He said something about having a drink with some old army buddies and he'd be back by midnight." She bent over to pick up the baby. "Oh, my dear," she murmured. "Wet to the skin. I'll give her a quick dip in the kitchen sink."

"Do that," Jeb said. "I'll see if I can stall whoever this is at the door. Gran?"

"Fast asleep. She wore herself out today."

"But enjoyed herself?"

"You ain't just whistlin' Dixie."

Their paths divided. Meg headed for the kitchen; Jeb whistled up Rex and started toward the front door. The dog was old, but not incapable, and when he opened his mouth and demonstrated those huge teeth it was enough to scare any dishonest citizen out of his skin. Or her skin. Lastly Jeb went by the gun-rack and picked up his favorite over-and-under shotgun. There was not a shell to be had to fit it, but then how was a stranger to know?

He flipped on the porch light and then unlocked the door. There was only one shadow out there in the darkness. Big Frank. Warily Jeb opened the door. Fangold brushed by him, and paused when Rex growled at him.

"Does he bite?" Frank asked cautiously.

"Only people I don't like," Jeb returned. "Or people he expects might do something mean."

"Hey, not me!"

Looking past Big Frank into the darkness of Virginia Street, Jeb could see the stretch limousine nosing in under the shadows of the trees. He closed the door and switched off the lights before he turned to the rotund little man.

"I invited you to lunch, not supper," he said. The shotgun under his arm swung casually around. Fangold raised both hands elbow-high.

"This is just a friendly social call," Frank said. "You invited me to see the baby. Here I am. I'm not looking for trouble—unless you can tell me where that stupid wife of mine is. If I get my hands on that dame, let me tell you there'll be trouble. And then some."

"I haven't any idea where your wife is," Jeb said. "In fact, I didn't even know you were married."

"What the hell?" Frank grunted. "You thought babies was brought in by the stork? So where's the baby?"

It was at that moment that Meg came in from the kitchen. Baby Eleanor was wrapped up in a huge bath towel, giggling away for all she was worth. All of her except her little round face was under cover. Fangold moved into the light, closer than Jeb really wanted him to be.

"Nice kid," Frank said, "but he sure doesn't look like anybody in my family. Course there ain't nobody left in my family but me and my wife and this boy."

"Girl," Meg corrected him. "And where did you say your wife was?"

"I didn't say," Frank said. "I don't know. She emptied the wall safe in our apartment before she went off to the hospital. And she never came back. Neither her nor the boy."

"Girl," Meg corrected him again.

"Listen," Frank said. "I gotta have a boy. You can't run no mob with a girl! I'd get laughed out of the Family." By that time he was close enough to Meg to touch. His fingers slipped through the folds of the towel.

"What do ya know?" he said grimly. "It *is* a boy!"

"It's a girl," Meg said very firmly. "Let go of my finger!"

There was a siren in the distance, rushing angrily over Cross Street, heading directly toward Virginia. "Damn, I gotta get out of here," Big Frank said. He started for the door. Rex threatened him with a couple of massive barks. Outside, somebody in the limousine blew a frantic horn and started the engine.

Fangold slammed through the door and almost fell down the stairs. Jeb went to the door to watch. Rex continued to bark—from behind Jeb's back. Meg joined the procession, keeping behind all the males of the house, but standing on tiptoes so she could see everything that went on.

"If he keeps on like that," she said, "all that eating and drinking and running up and down stairs, he's going to have a heart attack!"

The door of the limo slammed shut, and the driver backed madly toward the street. But the police car pulled up and blocked its way, and everything came unstuck.

Three policemen got out of the squad car. Two approached the limousine cautiously, hands on their weapons. The third bypassed the action and came up on to the porch. "Having a little trouble, are we?" Lieutenant Overton asked.

"Not really," Jeb said nervously, his voice wavering just the slightest bit. For no good reason at all he passed his shotgun over to the officer. "I still haven't had a chance to get any rock salt, so it's still empty. This is my fiancée."

"Meg Hubbard," the lieutenant said, putting out his hand. "I used to be her Sunday-school teacher years ago."

"And our baby, Eleanor," Meg said.

"Cute little thing," Overton remarked. "Doesn't look like either of your families. Well, we've had our eye on Big Frank ever since he came to town. We'll take him down to the station and have a little talk with him. But remember what I told you. Be careful. We can't watch over you all the time."

Jeb smiled, trying not to look too stupid, and closed the door behind the departing policeman.

"I am amazed at how much courage you have," Meg said softly as she brushed a kiss across his cheek. "I'm proud to know you."

Jeb shook his head and leaned back against the door. "Yeah," he returned sarcastically. "I'm so brave, aren't I? 'Let go of my finger!'"

"I had to say something," she insisted as she nestled a little closer.

"Why don't we go upstairs and I'll tell you just how brave you are?"

"You mean that?"

"Every word."

"What the devil is going on out here?" Annie Mae Hubbard demanded. Jeb groaned. He could feel another victory slipping slowly away from him.

CHAPTER EIGHT

HANDLING the heavy Cadillac on a day when tourists were beginning to flock into Urbanna was difficult, even for a man as big and well-muscled as Dixon. It was the day before the Oyster Festival, and the parade elements were out practicing.

"I haven't missed a parade in seventy-eight years," Annie Mae Hubbard told them all. Dixon was driving, Gran Hubbard sharing the front seat. Meg sat in back with the baby, and Jeb was beside her. By some miracle they had been able to find a parking space just a few steps from the Taber playground, and the paraders, who came up Marston Avenue, and then turned left on Rappahannock, marched right by their doors. "Although I never, ever had an air-conditioned seat," the old lady reflected. "You're a good boy, Jeb."

"Isn't he though?" Meg added. Eleanor merely gurgled. "Did you see many of the ladies from the garden club, Gran?"

"Practically everybody." A pause for reflection. "And you know something, Meg? I do believe a number of them were jealous!"

"You can't blame them for that," Meg returned as she hugged the baby close. "Can you?"

"No," the old lady said. "To tell the truth when I first met your Jeb I was a little jealous myself. When people get to be my age they sometimes say and do foolish things."

"But not you, Gran," Jeb said.

136

The old lady reached round and gave him a solid whack on the knee and then grinned at him. "Especially me, young man," she told him. "And now that you two are going to get married I think it's time for me to move back into my own home."

"Not if you don't want to," Jeb said. "There's always plenty of room with us down on Virginia Street. And you'll have more time to be with the baby."

"I appreciate that, but I know from experience how rotten things can be when you're living with your mother-in-law."

"Grandmother-in-law," Jeb corrected her. "There's a difference."

"Not much," Annie Mae said. "Don't try to kid me, son. I'm a mean, crotchety old woman. I've treated Meg like some kind of a slave girl. And now she has you. Which is about as much as any grandmother can ask."

"And did Mrs Brill agree to come and live with you?" Meg asked.

"Thanks to your paying her salary," Gran said, chuckling. "For a woman born and raised in Tappahannock she's proved to be a very capable cook. And she has a sister, I hear. Now how you both are going to get along without her I don't know. Meg can't cook worth a dime; but then I was sure she couldn't take care of a baby, either, and look at her!"

"I'd like to," Jeb teased, "but if I turn around to look at her now I'll miss half the parade practise, and Dixon might run over half the population of Middlesex County. They're all out in the middle of the street. Look at them!"

"The streets *are* a little crowded," Dixon said. "And the sidewalks too. Do you suppose there's anyone still at home between here and Richmond?"

By this time they had reached Cross Street, and were starting down the hill at Virginia. Surprisingly, there were a number of cars going the same way. "Windows restaurant," Meg said. "Down at the foot of the hill. They have a big feast on the boards today. And tomorrow they may have the oyster-shucking contest in front of the Windows parking lot. I understand the North American champion will be competing."

"Is that you?" Jeb asked.

"Me? I couldn't shuck an oyster if you paid the prize money in gold!"

"Well, it must be crowded down there," Gran said. "One of them is parking in our driveway."

Meg leaned over so that her lips were close to Jeb's ear. "And a Canadian license plate," she said softly. "Toronto, I believe."

"But Rex isn't barking," Jeb murmured. "Dixon?"

The burly butler slid out of his seat and stalked up the stairs. And only then did Rex begin to sound off. Dixon opened the front door of the house and then disappeared from sight. In a moment he came out and walked slowly down the stairs and over to the car. "A woman," he reported, leaning in the side window. "Tall, very thin, red hair. Claims to be your sister."

"Yes, I've got one of those." Jeb stepped out of the car and straightened out his shirt and tie. It was the first week in November, and winter was approaching from somewhere up in Yankee-land. Spurts of rain, cold spells, invigorating winds. But nothing of snow and ice. That might come later.

"Dixon, if you might help the ladies into the house?"

The bodyguard-butler nodded. Jeb shrugged. Yes, I've got one of those, he thought. And what trouble is she bringing our way now? Deep in the back of his mind was a thought about the baby. There was a quotation he remembered. "The Lord gave, and the Lord hath taken away; blessed be the name of the Lord." Baby Eleanor had arrived by his sister's hand—and what did she want now? A reward? A return?

Someone else was remembering that phrase too. There were footsteps just behind him, and the clack of high heels. "Meg?" he asked, not turning around.

"She wants *our* baby," Meg said desperately. "We have to do something to stop her! Money. She'll want money. Give her anything she wants—except our baby!"

Jeb nodded. The words rang in his ears. "Our baby!" And for a man whose romances had all been in his mind for years—or in his books—he was astonished at how much the idea of losing Eleanor hurt. We are three parts of the same person, he told himself grimly. Meg and Eleanor and I. We're a troika that can't be broken!

"Don't give up yet," he cautioned his fiancée. "If she wants money, we can bargain. And don't mention Big Frank, whatever you do!"

"Mention him? Good lord, I'm scared to death just thinking about him. Can't you do something to make him go away?"

"He's the one man we can't bribe," he said. "He's got more money than he knows what to do with. And more men to back him up than the entire police force in Urbanna.

"But look," he added, "there's a solution to every problem." He turned the knob and walked into the house. Rex played around his feet like a young puppy. The divan in the study squeaked as if someone was stretched out there.

"Well, it's about time somebody came home," his sister commented. Jeb walked through the doorway, but held up an arm to stop Meg in her tracks. My sister, he told himself. But Gwen looked like nothing he had ever seen before. She was dressed in a pair of baggy old coveralls. Her red hair hung down her back like a collection of strings. There were flecks of gray mixed with the red. Her face was lined, worn, as if life had suddenly overburdened her.

He suppressed the smart remarks that usually peppered his conversation with his sister. There were a lot of memories filling the spaces between himself and this woman. "Hello, Gwen," he said gently.

"Hello, little brother."

"Want something to eat?"

"I—don't think so. I haven't been well lately. My stomach's upset. It's a long drive down from the border."

"How about a bed and a bath?"

"Not just this minute."

I've never heard her so quiet, Jeb told himself. Not since we moved out of Richmond. Meg cleared her throat from behind him.

"Oh, yes. Gwen, this is my fiancée, Margarete Hubbard. We're planning to marry the day after tomorrow. It's good that you can be here."

Gwen shook her head. "I can't be here that long," she said, sighing. "I have a problem. A major problem."

"Money again?"

"Yes and no. It is, but it isn't. I'm broke. But I'm always broke, aren't I? It's been hard for two of us to live on my allowance, and then I have this bill." She reached into her purse, removed a paper, and handed it over.

"A funeral bill?"

Meg shook his arm, not too gently, and then walked by him and sat down next to his sister. Jeb looked more closely. For the first time since he could remember his sister was crying, and Meg was trying to comfort her.

"Totie didn't make it," Gwen managed to squeeze out between the tears.

"Totie?"

"Totie D'Amore. You must remember her? We went to school together. They used to live next door to us back in Richmond. She and I were best friends for a long time."

"Ah. That one!"

Meg got up and walked out into the kitchen, where her gran and Dixon and the baby had just come in. There was a buzz of conversation; orders were given in Meg's low voice, and then she came back into the study. This time she didn't pause. She went straight over to the liquor cabinet, poured a good-sized shot of brandy into a glass, and brought it over to the stricken woman.

"Here, drink this all down and then tell us about it," Meg commanded. Gwen took the glass thankfully and tossed the contents down her throat. She choked for a bit, then sat up straight and passed the empty glass back.

"Totie," she mused. "We graduated from school together, and then I didn't see her again for years. About a year ago I got a telephone call from her. She was living in New York, and said she desperately had to see me. I don't know how she got my telephone number, but she sounded so terrible that I went to see her. Is there more brandy?"

"There's plenty."

With glass refilled Gwen worked up her courage.

"Totie was always a very biddable girl. She was scared to death of her father, and when he ordered her to marry Frank Fangold she collapsed. They put in ten years of misery, and then she discovered that she was pregnant.

That was when she called on me for help." Gwen took a sip of brandy this time, rolling it over her tongue rather than swilling it all down.

"In any event, Totie convinced me she just had to get away from Big Frank and his family. Hell, I was so naive that I thought she really meant his family. But he didn't *have* a family. He only had a *Family*—you know... Mafia! In any event she waited until a day that her husband was out of town on business, then she cracked the family wall safe and the pair of us ran for Canada. It wasn't bad at first. The baby was born healthy, but Totie never did fully recover. She started to really go downhill about a month ago."

"So that's when you rushed down here and dumped the kid on me," Jeb interjected.

"So who else, dear brother? How is the kid, by the way?"

"The baby's fine," Meg said. "You waited a while to enquire, didn't you?"

"I'm not exactly fond of children," Gwen said. "Besides, with Big Frank's soldiers on my tail, I didn't have a lot of time to smell the roses."

"So then what happened?" Meg pushed.

"Not much. I went back up to Ontario, found a cheap boarding house just outside of Toronto, and Totie and I settled in. Unfortunately ten days later, to the day, she began to go downhill. Talked at me for hours, all about Frank and his Family. I thought I had it tough growing up, but Totie, she—oh, well, eventually she died. I had her buried in Sacred Heart cemetery, just outside of the city, and then started to look for help. Mother brushed me off, so I had to come back to Jeb again. He has the bill."

"It isn't much of a bill," Jeb said. "Naturally I'll pay it. But Gwen, what you don't seem to recognize is that Big Frank's people traced you and the baby right here to Urbanna. In fact, Frank is still in town. You're a lot less safe here than you were up in Canada."

"Oh, God," the woman groaned. "I'll have to get out of here. Where's my car?"

"You don't have the strength to drive as far as Perkins Creek," her brother said. "Now, we have a sort of fortress set-up here. I suggest that you get a shower, hit the sack, and get a lot of sleep. In the next two days of festival I don't think that Sherlock Holmes could track you down in the middle of Urbanna. Deal?"

Gwen gave him a positive shake of her head.

"The only other thought I have is after the festival you should pack up and visit Mother in Paris," Jeb continued. "She might not like it, but we won't give her any chance to wiggle out of it. How about that?"

"You really think she'd put herself out for me?"

"She's waiting for her monthly allowance. You'll bring it along with you. She'll welcome you like the flowers in spring."

"But the baby?" Meg said in a high-pitched worried voice. "I'm not going to give up our baby!"

"Not to worry," Jeb said. "We seem to be the only ones putting in a bid for the baby. Even Big Frank doesn't want her, if he's convinced that she's a girl. Now, Meg, you take my sister in hand. Dixon, get Gertrude busy hunting up some clothes Gwen might wear."

"Share and share alike," Meg demanded. "What are *you* going to do?"

"Fair's fair," her fiancé announced grandly. "I'm going to look after the baby! And Mrs Brill will be packing up to move to Gran's house tomorrow. And Annie Mae, of course, will supervise!''

"You know," Gwen mused, "it's hard for a girl to grow up with a little brother tagging after her. When you were a little kid I never thought you'd amount to anything at all."

"And what do you know?" Jeb said, with a long face. "You were right!"

Meg stuck out her tongue at both of them, then towed Gwen upstairs and out of sight.

The Oyster Festival seemed to have started before sunrise. Because of the packed sidewalks and streets Jeb left the driving to Dixon when it was time for Annie Mae to move back to her own house. Everywhere in town—along the streets, in all the parking lots, along the piers—there were oysters, crabs, clams, Polish sausages, clam necks and gallons of cider, all awaiting their fate.

The official festival opened at ten o'clock in the morning, but by that time Gran was back in her home on Kent Street, the bands were playing all over town, and the carnival tents were full to bursting out at the playground. Down by the waterfront a pair of tall ships were tied up, available to tourists, and the coast guard had doubled its participation, just in case.

By one o'clock that afternoon the town was rocking. Meg had settled Gran down in her own house with Mrs Brill in attendance and then had come back to Virginia Street; Dixon had parked the Cadillac and Gwen's rental car behind the house and had gone down to the waterfront to enjoy the remainder of his day. Gertrude was walking out with her young man.

"I don't remember ever being that young," Meg said as she watched the maid go down the stairs. "You?"

"Me?" Jeb slouched back on the divan and put his feet up. "It seems to me I was always older than that. As the only boy in the family I was born old. Where's my sister?"

"Still asleep," Meg reported. "Woke up at eight o'clock, just as we were making our first trip over to Gran's house. I fed her bacon and eggs and waffles with blueberries, and she promptly went back to bed again. She says she doesn't intend to go out on the streets until she's sure that Big Frank has gone back home."

"So now what?"

"Hey, this is celebration time. The town is full to overflowing. They have clowns and acrobats along all the streets, there's enough food being sold to feed a battleship crew and—here we sit. You and me and Eleanor."

"And tomorrow is the fatal day," Jeb said.

"I don't look on marriage as being fatal. I'm sort of—looking forward to it," Meg replied.

"Me too," Jeb said. "So, there's only the pair of us—and our daughter—in the house. Why don't we slip upstairs and find something interesting to do?"

"With a leer like that you could be Groucho Marx. Don't forget that your sister's upstairs. Any little noise will wake her up, I'm sure."

"Damn!" Jeb stood up, just in time to accidentally wake Eleanor. Meg got up, smiling at the frustrated look on his face.

"Jeb Lacey," she said, "you have a one-track mind. So why don't we take our daughter out strolling in her new carriage and see what's to be seen?"

"Isn't that something? You and me and our daughter." Jeb stretched and watched as Meg picked up the baby. "Look at me," he said. "Not more than six weeks ago

I was a happy bachelor and you were writing for the local magazine. And now there's a hot time in town and all we can think to do is take our daughter out and walk the streets.''

And so they went walking. Out into the sunshine, up the hill toward Cross Street, past the old Lansdowne house just next to the relatively new post office, where a pair of strolling jugglers were entertaining, and——

''Look,'' Meg said, pointing up the street. ''Frank Fangold. And one of his—what do you call them? Henchmen? Minions? And he's driving himself. I wonder if he knows how potent that cider is? And how in the world did he get that big limousine up the street on a day like this?''

Jeb, who was chief engineer in charge of carriage-pushing, looked up and barely caught a glimpse. ''Never mind the limousine! How in the world did he get that big stomach through the crowd? What's he doing now?''

''He's going up the street, eating. Stopping at most every booth, cramming down whatever they're serving. That man must weigh two hundred and fifty pounds!''

''And only five feet six, or something like that. A hundred pounds overweight, would you say?''

''At least.''

So, like a pair of conspirators, they ducked down Prince George Street, only to meet Big Frank again, not three blocks away, still eating. And when they turned off on Rappahannock Avenue some time later there was Big Frank one more time, still eating.

''And speaking of eating, it's about time for Eleanor's bottle,'' Meg said. ''Besides which, my feet hurt.''

''Yeah,'' Jeb said, looking down at the blisters forming on the palms of both hands. ''So why don't we quit and go home?''

So the Lacey family turned back down Virginia, and took refuge in what all three of them had begun to think of as home. The house was as quiet as a church home—except that somewhere upstairs Gwen was snoring away, but ladylike, of course, as befitting a Wormeley of the first families of Virginia.

The baby was ready to quit for the afternoon. Meg took her upstairs and bedded her down in her crib. "All that fresh air wore the little tyke out completely," she said as she came back downstairs into the study. "She's out like a light. And your sister isn't doing too much better! That woman is going to sleep the week away. Ah, you're working! We aren't going to starve to death after all."

Jeb looked up and smiled at her. "Don't count on it. But I've come up with a fine ending for *The Baby Caper*, and I've got a proposal running around in my head about watermen and oysters."

"Never will amount to anything," Meg said as she plumped herself down on the divan and picked up the newspaper. "You can't write a successful book about a subject that you hate."

"And don't count on *that* either," Jeb said as his fingers felt tentatively toward the keys, pecked out a couple of words, and then moved into high speed.

It was no use trying to get his attention when he was off, hot on the trail of some story, Meg knew.

"There's an army of blue shell crabs climbing up Virginia Street," she coaxed.

"Uh-huh."

"They're eating the library."

"Uh-huh."

"The moon is falling."

"How nice."

Meg kicked her shoes off and threw the newspaper onto the floor. "I'd sure like a little lovin'!"

The chatter of the keyboard stopped in midstream. The wheels on his computer chair squeaked. One click of a switch signified the defeat of the machine. And the cushions on the divan sank with an explosion of air as he skidded over the floor and came down beside her.

"You'd sure like—what?"

"A little lovin'," she repeated softly. "I don't mind if the dog watches."

"Well, I do," he gruffed. "Rex. Go!" The ancient animal glared at him, but struggled up and made his way out to the kitchen, where food and water waited. "Old age sets in," Jeb said. "He'd rather eat than love."

"And you? You're no spring chicken."

"I don't believe in boasting *before* the performance," he said as he reached out for her.

She came willingly.

Meg sighed. "I didn't know it could be so—interesting," she said softly.

"Nor I that you would respond so—delightfully," he said, chuckling. They were lying on the floor as close together as two people possibly could get, she tastefully nude, he wearing nothing but his blue and yellow socks. One of his hands cupped her breast, still weighing, testing, satisfying. "We have to be careful about floor burns," he added.

"Floor burns? I knew we had to be careful about something, but floor burns?"

"The carpet isn't thick enough," he said. "We should have gone upstairs. But not to worry about that other. I don't suppose you're on the Pill?"

"Me? I never thought—I hadn't been planning for this to—— No. No pills."

"And besides," he commented, "we're getting married tomorrow. Would you object to another child?"

"No," she said tentatively. "That's another thing I haven't given much thought to. Did you plan to fill the house? If so I'd rather we moved to a smaller place."

"Coward."

"Inexperienced," she fought back. "I know—I think I know what births are all about, but—I do wish you'd stop doodling with my—with me. If you mean to do it again, then do it, but don't just be a tease!"

"You wouldn't mind?"

"I'm crazy to have you do it again, you fool," she said as she rolled over on top of him and bounced gently against him. At least that's something he can't dawdle about, she told herself. Just touch him in the right place—places?—and he's instantly aroused. Massively aroused. All she really knew about men came from that nude statue of Apollo, up in Richmond. And the statue was certainly not in the same class as Jeb Lacey.

"Maybe we *should* go upstairs," she suggested. "The baby won't be awake for another hour, and we could——"

"Yes, we certainly could," he agreed as he helped her to her feet. "At least once."

"And that's all?" Meg slung her blouse over her shoulder and bundled up the rest of her clothes. Jeb picked up his undershorts and left everything else on the floor.

"Hey, lady, whoa up. I do the best I can, but I'm no machine. I'm glad to see that you're a tiger——"

"Tigress," she corrected.

"Tigress in this sort of work, but there has to be some rationing now and again."

"But you said when we started off—something about you could do this all day and all night? I distinctly remember!"

"Fiction," he acknowledged. "What I really said was that I would *like* to be *able* to do it all day——"

"And all night," she teased.

"And all night." He accepted the compromise, put one arm around her, and started for the stairs. "You don't bounce a lot," he said as they reached the third stair.

"Oh? The women you're accustomed to, they bounce a great deal?"

"Well, I—you know—I mean when they're—walking, or running, and you don't——"

"Oh, I bounce with the best of them when I'm running," she said. "But I don't dare to run up the stairs. It might wear you out. Tell me about all these bouncy women you know."

"Nobody likes a smart alec," he grumbled, and then moved over closer to Meg as someone else was trying to come down the stairs! Gwen!

"And what have we here?" his sister asked archly. "Dear conservative, old-fashioned Jeb. Getting married tomorrow, and tearing off a sample tonight?"

Jeb fumbled for a word or two. Meg provided them. "Aw, shut up," she snapped. "Stop picking on your brother. He deserves everything he can get. And I'm glad to provide it."

She wanted to say a thousand other things as well, but Jeb took her arm and hurried her up the rest of the stairs and into his bedroom. Behind them they could hear Gwen's laugh, low and cracked and bitter.

"I could easily hate that woman," Meg said as she clung to Jeb, standing in the middle of the room.

"I do sometimes myself," he responded. "But then I just recall some of the things she had to put up with and I feel sort of guilty myself."

"What are you saying, Jeb? That there's some perfectly good reason for her to act the way she does? Nothing could be that——"

"Wait, Meg."

"Wait? I feel like going back downstairs and punching her in the mouth. She could wreck our marriage, and I can't put up with that."

"Wait," he repeated, speaking very slowly and deliberately. "My father used to abuse her."

"What?"

"You heard me. I didn't find out about it until I was sixteen."

"And you? Did he abuse you too? Is that why you're so wrapped up in your books?"

Jeb chuckled. "When I was sixteen," he said, "I was five inches taller than my father, and outweighed him by twenty pounds. I can't say that he never had an effect on me, but it was easier for him to pick on Gwen."

"But you did something—when you were sixteen?"

"Yes, I did something. I beat the living hell out of him and threw him out of the house. I haven't seen him since. And my mother, she hasn't really spoken to me since. He was only funning, she said. It was a phase. It would wear off. She loved him very much. And can you guess what else?"

"Not too hard," Meg said. "He also abused your mother? Well, that's what you might expect, love. He hated women."

"I don't know about that. When Gwen and I moved away that was the last I ever heard of the man."

"You moved out? And then what did you do?"

"I had inherited a little money from my grandfather. So I took it, and moved Gwen and myself to Richmond. And yes, we all are marked by him. That's one of the reasons we're such a crazy crew. You're the first normal person to come into the Lacey family in over twenty years. I'm very grateful to you, Meg."

"Please—don't use that word. I don't want a grateful husband. I want a man who is firm, sincere and knows his own mind. And I think you're it."

"I don't suppose you'd care to renew our little game?" He made a gesture toward the bed.

"I don't think so, Jeb. Not until tomorrow. But I would like to lie down and rest. The pair of us together, just to rest?"

"That I can do," he said as he led her over to the bed, opened it up, and helped her climb under the sheets. She lay flat on her back, hands folded behind her head, and smiled at him for the first time that evening. He studied her as she lay there, outlined by the pure white sheets. At least I know her better, he thought. All those curves are not just promises, not now.

"Things aren't so bad," she told him. "Every family has some sort of defect in it. I'm glad you told me about the Laceys. It's not something I would like to stumble on some time after our marriage."

"Then the marriage is still on?"

"Of course. I love you very much, Mr Lacey, and just because your sister caught us skinny-dipping it doesn't mean I'm going to—to break up a beautiful wedding. Now, no more talk. Hold my hand and close your eyes.

We both will need a large amount of courage in order to face tomorrow."

He kissed her gently and stretched out beside her. Through the open bedroom window he could hear the festival in full swing. When he looked at Meg again she had fallen asleep. But she was smiling.

CHAPTER NINE

ON SATURDAY Mother Nature was not too interested in providing comfort for the rest of the festival. Sullen clouds hung over the entire area. Thunder bowled its warning from time to time. By ten in the morning, when the clog dancers were scheduled to begin up at the playground, rain came down in bucketfuls. And then, when it thought it had done enough, the clouds rolled down the Chesapeake and out to sea. By eleven o'clock the streets had dried, but puddles of mud still spotted the festival grounds, and the oyster-shucking competition was going full speed.

Meg stalked up and down over at her gran's house, worry-lines deep on her face. "But Gran——"

"There's no hope, lass. I cannot possibly walk you down the aisle with this—affliction in me. I've already spent the morning sitting in the bathroom. No hope for it—you need a substitute."

"Maybe I could help?" Gwen, finally coaxed out of the house on Virginia Street, made a tentative offer. The look on her face showed she hoped the offer would be refused.

"Oh, lord, yes," Meg said, grabbing at her arm. "All you have to do is walk down the aisle with me, and catch me if I decide I'd rather run than marry."

Gwen grinned at her. "There's a chance of that? You'd really leave my little brother standing at the altar?"

"Of course I wouldn't," Meg said. "What woman would?"

"I did once," Gwen said. "And he was the most handsome man I'd ever met. I don't know what came over me. Fear of the unknown, I guess. That was seven years ago. I'd give everything I own to be able to try again. You remember Wendell Stuart, Annie Mae?"

"I remember," she said. "A fine-looking young man. Had only one trouble, as I remember. He was chronically unemployed. The boy is still around town, to the best of my knowledge."

"And still unemployed?" Gwen asked.

"I don't know about that," Annie Mae said. "There was some talk about him joining the police force. They don't pay a lot, but it's steady work." Her old clock began to strike the hour. "By this time," she added, "you people should be going up the steps at the church. Instead you're three blocks away. Well!"

The house was filled with female screams. Even Eleanor added her bit. And out of all the confusion they finally ran for the Cadillac, where Dixon, a man of great patience—after all, it wasn't *he* who was getting married—sat behind the wheel, the motor quietly turning over, listening to music on the FM radio band. "The church, ma'am?"

"Dear lord, yes. Get me to the church on time."

"It would take a miracle," the big butler muttered as he checked that all the doors were closed, then pulled gently away from the curb. It was eleven ten, and the parade wasn't scheduled to pass that point until one o'clock.

"Where the hell are they?" Jeb Lacey asked as he checked his watch for the third time. "You don't suppose she——? No, she wouldn't do that."

"They'll be along in their own good time," Elmer
Carter said. Elmer was a waterman, an old friend who,
whenever Jeb took a break from his writing, provided
the boat, the know-how, the bait and the encouragement
to get him out on the water. They had served in the
military together during the Gulf War. Only now, Elmer
told himself as he tugged at his too tight collar, there
are lots of things I don't understand about weddings.

Surprisingly, exactly the same thought was running
through the mind of the Reverend Stanton, whose church
had, on more than one occasion, seen a backward bride
who refused at the final moment to take the plunge. The
good Reverend cleared his throat, checked his notes on
the marriage service, and signaled to Mrs Raeburn, who
not only served the Veterans of Foreign Wars Women's
Auxiliary, but also played the organ—enthusiastically—
whenever required. The organ burped, music filled the
church, and a Cadillac pulled up at the front door.

"There," the Reverend said, pointing down the aisle.
The little group waiting at the altar straightened up.
Carter fumbled in his vest pocket to be sure of the ring—
for the fifth time—and the processional swelled up and
out, startling even the tourists who had come for the
oyster stew, and were just as pleased to eat while the
bride walked down the aisle.

The small bridal party formed up in the outer lobby.
Meg, in her moment of glory, wore a plain white lace
dress, with sequined ribbons. The combination of silk
and satin over a taffeta slip rustled as she moved. The
dropped torso cascaded down to her knees, and then
flared out to almost brush the floor. The puff sleeves
gave her a place to tuck her handkerchief, and somehow
or another she felt she might need that protection. A

tiny pearl-beaded white cap supported her half-veil. Gran had insisted.

Gwen, the last-minute substitute bridesmaid, wore a two-piece dress in refreshing mint. The tunic top was styled in a round neckline, while the pull-on skirt featured softly pleated double tiers.

Dixon, a volunteer in a male-short household, came to "give her away" dressed, as were the two men waiting at the altar, in dark tailed morning coat and dove-grey trousers and vest, with a boutonniere in his lapel. But nobody had come to look at the men. Well, almost nobody.

Mrs Raeburn thumped on the organ a time or two to get up speed, and the solemn Wedding March began to ring out through the neighborhood. Dixon offered his arm, and the cortege started down the aisle.

And my voyage begins, Meg told herself. Twenty-eight years I've been growing toward this time and place— and this man. Her throat was dry as dust. I should have brought a lozenge, she thought. Step, stop, step, stop, step. Dixon tugged at her arm.

"Halfway down the aisle," he whispered. "Last chance, if you want to run." She looked up at him, startled. He was smiling. Well, actually, he was laughing. She mustered up her own grin and maneuvered the last twenty feet almost dancing. Dixon slowed her to a stop, took a moment to fold her veil up out of the way, kissed her cheek, and passed her hand over to Jeb. Who was so nervous that he almost dropped it. Meg passed her bouquet to Gwen. Dixon moved aside to sit in the first pew. The four members of the party—the bride, groom, bridesmaid and best man—turned to face the altar. Meg took a deep breath and held it.

"Friends," the pastor said, "we are gathered together in the sight of God to witness and bless the joining together of Margarete Mary and John Egemont Basil in Christian marriage."

Who? Meg asked herself. Have they rung in a substitute for Jeb? John Egemont Basil? She looked over at him. He stood so solemnly and stiffly that it appeared he might break in two. John Egemont Basil? And yet he looked like Jeb. Dear lord! It took an effort to suppress her giggles.

"The covenant of marriage was established by God, who created us male and female for each other," the pastor went on. "Jesus gave us the example for the love of husband and wife when he graced the wedding at Cana in Galilee. Now Margarete and John come to give themselves to one another in this holy covenant."

Hold on, Meg thought. Where would we be if a big ox like me were to faint and fall down on the floor? Her hand, resting gently on Jeb's arm, tightened. Jeb looked over at her, perturbed, and took some of her weight to himself.

Some of what the pastor said slipped completely over Meg's head until he turned directly to her. "Margarete, will you have John to be your husband, to live together in holy marriage? Will you love him, comfort him, honor and keep him, in sickness and in health, and, forsaking all other, be faithful to him as long as you both shall live?"

Of course I will, Meg thought. That's what it's all about. Why are they all staring at me? The pastor smiled, and nodded at her. Jeb tugged gently at her hand. You forgot, she told herself, blushing. "I will."

More conversation between the Reverend and—John. "I will," he said.

Jeb had his part down pat. I wish I were that smart, Meg thought. And it was time to say, "In the name of God, I Margarete take you John to be my husband, to have and to hold from this day forward, for better, for worse, for richer, for poorer, in sickness and in health, to love and to cherish until death us do part. This is my solemn vow."

And then it was time to exchange rings. Elmer Carter fumbled madly, and couldn't find the one entrusted to him for the longest time. Jeb glared at him. But eventually things worked out well, and together they and the congregation said the Lord's Prayer. Far in the rear of the church Baby Eleanor, who had had enough of all this folderol, began to complain, first in a subdued tone, and then as loudly as she could go.

The good Reverend, who had four children of his own, speeded up the procedure. "God the Eternal keep you in love with each other, so that the peace of Christ may abide in your home. Go forth to serve God—and your neighbor—in all that you do. The peace of the Lord be with you always."

And the entire congregation added, "And also with you."

"Now kiss the girl," the Reverend Stanton ordered, "before kissing goes out of style."

And Mrs Raeburn and her organ thundered majestically as everyone got up, milled about, and went to the lobby to congratulate the newlyweds.

The wedding reception was scheduled for the old customs house, Jeb's old house on Virginia Street. Ordinarily Jeb would have booked a restaurant, but on festival day none was available. And at one o'clock sharp the festival parade would start. Which meant that approximately one hundred people, now standing in the

outer lobby of the church, would be completely trapped
as the paraders marched around them, like a horde of
Indians isolating a wagon train.

"So I hired three school buses," Jeb explained to the
congregation. "Leave your cars here, and when you're
ready to go home I suspect the festival will be settled
down, at which time I'll have a couple of rented cars to
bring you all back here a family at a time, to pick up
your own vehicles. Here come the buses!"

"I don't know how you do it," Meg whispered to him.
Since the moment when the good Reverend had told him
to kiss her she had been trapped under his right arm,
and he was making no effort at all to release her.

"Do what?" he asked. "Kiss the bride?"

"No, I mean the buses and the food and the routes
to avoid the parade, and——"

"What I *don't* understand," he said, "is how I get us
off by ourselves, with all this crowd of people, so that,
now that I've got a license for it, we can go do what
comes naturally!"

"What's all that mean?" she teased. "That same old
subject?"

"You'd better believe it," he threatened. "Doesn't it
ever cross your mind?"

"Constantly," she said, blushing rose-red. "I'm sure
we can find a way, after a while."

"After a while," he grumbled. "That's what bothers
me. Come on, Pocahontas; we don't ride the bus; we
take the Cadillac."

They almost made it. The church grounds took up
almost the entire city block, with the rectory at one side,
an expanse of parking lots at the middle and the church
on the other. The buses pulled out onto Marston Avenue,
preparing to turn down Cross Street. Dixon brought the

Cadillac up to the door. Meg and Gwen and Carter and Jeb, holding the baby, crowded in, and just as they were about to move away a sound like ten thousand sirens split the air and two police cars skidded into the parking lot. Other sirens could be heard down the street.

Out of the first car stepped Lieutenant Overton. "It never rains but it pours," he said. "Miss Hubbard——"

"Mrs Lacey," Jeb interjected. "The service is over. We're serving cake and cuisine down on Virginia Street."

"And I'm serving trouble and terror up at the fair-grounds. I need both of you—Mr and Mrs Lacey. Now."

"What?"

"It's an emergency," the lieutenant repeated. "Your car?" He pointed toward the Cadillac.

"Our car?" Jeb questioned.

"Well, follow me, before we all get caught up in that damned parade."

"Parade," Jeb groaned. "I thought we had—— Look, I just got married, and there's a hundred people down at my house waiting to celebrate—and we've got the baby in this car..." Lieutenant Overton glared at him. "OK. Follow you."

Jeb climbed back into the Cadillac. Baby Eleanor gurgled at him. "Dixon, follow the cops—thataway." And away they went—thataway. "I don't know," Jeb told his brand-new wife. "The police department is out of its everloving mind. Follow me? They must think they're General Patton's army. Or somebody."

"Did you see who was driving that other police car?" his sister Gwen asked. There was a breathless quality to her question.

"Me? No," Jeb said. "Somebody you know?"

Gwen settled back comfortably in her seat, with a half-smile on her face. "Wendell," she said. "Wendell Stuart, and wearing sergeant's stripes on his arm."

"Wendell? The boy you almost——?"

"And he's employed, brother. Something you said could never happen. Never. Remember? What do you think of that?"

"As little as possible," Jeb returned. "I've made mistakes on occasions. Oh, Gawd, look at that!"

They and the police car had just turned west on Rappahannock Avenue. Up ahead, on the right, was the Taber playground, where the tents and concessions of the festival were set up. Farther ahead, on Route 602, just past the fire house, the head section of the parade—band, clowns, politicians—which was supposed to continue on south along the route and then circle up Cross Street, by the church, and come up behind the police cars, had broken off by some monumental mistake, had turned east on Rappahannock, and was confronting the racing police cars—and the Cadillac—face to face.

Brakes squealed. The leading police car fishtailed, and came to a stop with its nose just an inch or two away from the drum major. The band was playing "Stars and Stripes Forever"; it fell into a few miscellaneous squeaks and ground itself into silence.

"I need a drink," Elmer Carter said. "Are you sure we're going the right way?"

"Look ahead at the corner," Dixon said as he brought the Cadillac to a smooth halt.

"That's your friend Wendell," Jeb said glumly. "If he keeps driving like that for very long he'll be unemployed again. What do you see ahead, Dixon?"

"There's been an accident at the corner," Dixon reported. "I can't see it all, but there's a fire truck, one of those big decorated garbage trucks and a gray stretch limousine.''

"Oh, lord," Meg muttered. "Gray stretch limousine? He can't catch up to us, can he?"

"He who?" Gwen asked as she leaned anxiously toward the window.

"Not to worry," Dixon reported. "The limousine has its radiator a good two feet into a telephone pole. He must have been going like a bat out of hell. Looks as if there was a fire of some sort. And somebody hit the garbage truck. They're trying to tow it out of the way."

"Who?" Gwen insisted anxiously. "Who owns the limousine?"

"Big Frank Fangold," Jeb told her.

"Fangold? You mean Fangolio, don't you? Dear God, I've got to get away from here. Now!" Tears were forming in her eyes as she leaned back against the seat. Meg put an arm around her, comforting her. "Don't worry about him," she said. "Jeb can take care of him. He's done it two or three times already."

"There's really no place for us to go," Jeb said. "Here come the cops. Maybe we'll find out something from them." And sure I can take care of Big Frank, he told himself. Easy. The man's a killer. I'll shoot him to death with one of my drawing pencils? I love you very much, Meg Lacey, but don't set me up as a target for Big Frank! I'm not all *that* brave.

Lieutenant Overton was outside his window. Jeb rolled it down and stuck his head out. "Accident," the officer reported. "In back of all those carnival tents is an emergency hospital tent. That's where we're going. You'll have to get out and walk."

"That may be where *you're* going," Jeb responded, "but my wife is still outfitted in all her bridal gear, including high heels, and I'm not even going to let her *try* to walk all that way. Have another thought."

"Look," the lieutenant said, "this is all for your benefit. I don't exactly know what's going on, but one of my officers is over there. He called in on the radio. The surgeon says that they need you urgently."

"Need me? All my family is here in this car, except for my mother. And as far as I know she's in Paris. France, that is."

"All right, all right. Driver?"

Dixon turned around in his seat.

"Can you drive this—this car off the side of the road there?"

"I can if somebody gets the band to move," Dixon answered. Overton pulled down the little radio transceiver pinned to his shoulder, and had a muffled conference with his subordinates. He concluded the conversation with a muttered curse.

"You wouldn't believe it," he said. "They've got the garbage truck out of the ditch and now it's rolled sidewise across the highway and is blocking everything in sight. And the mayor is raising—the roof."

"Good lord," Jeb said, shaking his head. "The next thing you know they'll be running an elephant into the parade."

"Not today," the lieutenant said. "Although I heard it discussed in the planning session last summer. It seems there was a circus up at Richmond that went bankrupt. The carnival people here wanted to make a deal with somebody in the Chamber of Commerce to rent the beast for the festival. Thank God it wasn't even brought to a vote.

"Now then——" he turned back to Dixon "—can you drive this car around that band?"

"Just get them off to the side of the road," Dixon said. "I haven't seen an elephant up close since I was twelve years old. That would have been some attraction. Move the band."

"I think maybe I'd rather walk," Meg said hesitantly. She still had one arm around Gwen. Now Jeb's arm came around her shoulders.

"Courage, fortitude," he said as he patted her.

"I'm not Carlotta," she told him fiercely. "But I could easily murder the Grand Duke of Moldavia if you keep treating me like somebody's lost baby!"

"Who?" Gwen asked. "What?"

Fifteen minutes later the two newlyweds were still squabbling as the big car pulled up beside the tent farthest back in the playground. A Red Cross flag was flying over its entrance, and the rescue truck normally stationed at the fire house was parked alongside.

A parade of people was already moving in and out of the shelter. "I'll go in," Jeb said. "Looks like it's cuts and bruises day at the festival."

"I'll go with you," Meg added. "I'm not sure you could remember your head if it wasn't fastened on."

"What a nice thing to say," Jeb mourned. "Do we have to file for divorce before nightfall?"

"Gwen, would you hold the baby?" Meg asked.

"Me?"

"Well, she don't mean me," Elmer contributed. "Lord, I need a smoke."

"At the medical station?" Gwen asked sarcastically.

"Not with my baby in there," Meg said as she squeezed her way out of the car. "Nobody? All right, I'll take the baby with me!"

So three watched while the other three moved smartly into line and went into the tent. A volunteer nurse in uniform stood just inside the door. Her uniform was rumpled, and she already looked tired. Without looking up she whipped out a form. "Nature of injury?"

"Lacey," Meg said.

"Lacey? I don't have that on the form. Are you one of the entertainers?"

"No, I'm Lacey, and I've just come from my wedding and the police said——"

"Oh. Him? Go through that flap in back; there's a little anteroom and the doctor is back there. But you'd better hurry. There's a little mud back there. Be careful or you'll ruin your nice dress."

"I'm hurrying," Meg snapped.

Jeb caught up with her. "Let me have the little bit," he offered. His wife of two hours glared at him.

"I'll take care of the baby. Just find out what the devil is——"

Lieutenant Overton finally joined them. "Through here," he said, holding back the canvas screen that blocked off the back room. Meg gave him a brilliant thank-you smile and went on in. The others followed along behind. Dr Switzer, whom they had met when Gran Hubbard was hospitalized, was busy scribbling on a paper fastened to a clipboard. In back of him was a wheeled gurney, and behind that, up against the back wall of the tent, a small desk held a beeping heart monitor. Little lines of heartbeats ran irregularly across the face of the screen.

Wendell Stuart came in behind them with his own clipboard. All attention moved to him.

"The patient was driving the limo," he reported. "According to witnesses he was going over forty miles an hour, and heading directly into the front of the parade. Another witness said he stopped at four different food stands on his way up here, and drank cider at each one of them.''

"Cider? That can't hurt him," Meg said. "That's only apple juice."

Both policemen looked at her and Stuart said, ''What do you know? There's cider and then there's cider. And if you freeze it enough it's called Apple Jack!''

Meg blushed and clamped both her lips shut. She had heard the word more than once before. From Gran Hubbard, for a fact.

Stuart grinned at her, found his place and continued his report. ''He hit the garbage truck which was supposed to block off the entrance into Rappahannock Avenue, and then bounced into the telephone pole. Something under the hood caught fire, and the pumper truck responded from the fire station. The rescue crew got him out of the car before the fire got to him, and brought him here.''

Dr Switzer looked up from his paper. ''I don't think that's all, Overton,'' he said. ''There's every indication that he had a stroke before the accident. May have *caused* the accident, for that matter.''

"But this place is designed for Band-Aids and bruises," Jeb commented. "Why didn't the rescue squad take him directly to the hospital?''

"Because I don't dare to move him farther," the doctor said glumly. "He's all banged up inside. If I could get a helicopter—but I can't. Has that guy Racey showed up yet?''

"Lacey," Jeb insisted. "Lacey. That's me. Who is the patient?''

"Frank Fangold," Wendell Stuart said.

"Something like that," the doctor agreed. "Ate too much, drank too much, exercised too little. It could have happened to most anybody in that condition."

"Prognosis?" Overton asked.

"Ten percent chance of survival," the doctor said. "Lord, I'm tired. Stacey?"

"Yeah, that's me," Jeb said, tired of the battle over names.

"He wants something either from or for you," the doctor said. "He's able to talk intermittently, but not for long. You'd better get as close as you can."

Jeb reached out for Meg's hand. She took his, all the animosity gone from her face. Regardless of the man and her experience with him, he was real, and deserved sympathy. Jeb felt a little different. To him Frank Fangold was like a big rattlesnake, able to bite, prepared to bite, no matter who had stepped on his tail. So he weaved his way through the group and towed Meg along with him to the bundle that was all that was left.

Frank Fangold was not tall, but he was wide and deep, and he took up all the space there was on the gurney. A sheet covered him to the shoulders. There was a tube in his right arm leading up to a bag above his head. There was a needle in his left arm leading through a miscellany of wires to the heart monitor. And that weak, irregular beeping continued. Jeb coughed. Frank opened one eye and tracked Meg's movement as she came over to him. He moistened his lips a couple of times.

"Pretty lady," he said, and then coughed. Dr Switzer came immediately to join them.

"Coughing's bad," the doctor said.

"No time," Frank said. His voice was weak and fragile. His body, after the coughing spell, was fixed in position. Only his one open eye traced the pattern of the people looking down at him. "Pretty lady," he repeated. "Got married, did you?"

Meg leaned over him. "Yes, we got married. Just an hour ago."

"Nice," Frank said. "I done it all wrong. Totie never could of made it Italian style. Nice lady. I wish—where is she now, d'you suppose?"

Meg fished in her memory for all the answers that were needed. "Totie's dead," she told him softly. His other eye flew open.

"Dead? I never meant—— Where?"

"In Canada, Frank. Gwen had her buried in the Sacred Heart Cemetery, just outside of Toronto."

"Priest and all?"

"Priest and all, Frank."

"That's good. She deserved better. Her mother would like to know that."

A fit of coughing seized and shook him. When it was over his eyes closed. Jeb looked up at the doctor, who gestured toward the heart monitor. The man's pulse was struggling, but still functional. Dr Switzer shrugged.

And then his right eye opened again. "What killed her?" Frank asked. "I hope it wasn't me. I never meant to do that."

"The baby was too much for her."

"Ah. The baby. Totie always had a weakness for pain. I shouldn't of—it was all my doing. I thought I needed a boy to—— Where's the baby?"

"Right here." Meg unfolded the corner of the blanket which had fallen over Eleanor's face. The baby was awake, her eyes shining, her several teeth gleaming in the poor light in the shelter. She looked at her real father and gurgled.

Frank moistened his lips again. A nurse came over, held a straw to his lips, and fed him a drop or two of water. He managed, somehow, to swallow it all. "Got to be done right," he muttered. His voice level was dropping off, hardly as loud now as the beep of the monitor. "Name. Got to have a name."

"Her mother named her Eleanor," Jeb said.

"Totie's mother's name," Frank whispered. "Be sure you tell her. Middle?"

"Frank, we thought she ought to be named after both of you and after us. Suppose we have her christened Eleanor Frances? Eleanor Frances Lacey."

"You're not gonna put her in no home or nothin'?"

"Only in *our* home. As if she were our daughter."

"Good. Where's Murphy—that kid I sent down here? He's got all my money, the punk."

"He's outside," the policeman said.

"Bring him in," Frank gasped. "He ain't a bad punk. Could'a' been a nice kid."

"We don't need any money," Jeb assured him. "We have enough for all of us. And for Eleanor Frances."

"Eleanor Frances." Big Frank Fangold savored the name, tasted it a time or two. "Nice," he said, and his eyes closed again. A rictus of pain contorted his face.

"I ain't gonna make it, am I, Doc?"

"I don't suppose," Dr Switzer said. "There's nothing we could do."

"S'all right," the big man muttered. "I ain't been to church in thirty years, and now the priest came for me and all, and said the last rites, and Totie's in Canada?" As he paused the young man, one of the two who had rowed that boat across the cove, came in and stood by the gurney.

"Yes, Totie's in Canada," Meg said. "She's in God's hands."

"My mother used to talk like that," Frank said. His voice faded away to almost nothing, and then came back. "Take care of our daughter, Lacey. She deserves better than me. Tell the kid—some day, when she gets old enough to understand—that Big Frank loved her. I wanna be..." And the voice faded again.

"You want what, Frank?"

"Murphy, see if you can put me down beside Totie. She was a nice kid. An' one more thing."

"What's that?" Meg and Jeb both leaned down closer to the gurney. The man's voice was almost completely gone, but his face lit up as he made another effort. "Eleanor Frances. Listen, I give my baby to the pair of you. Take good care. I'll be watchin'."

"We will," Meg said. Her hand reached out to the man and touched him gently on his bare shoulder. "And then——"

Dr Switzer put a hand on Meg's. For the first time she heard the silence. The beeper had stopped.

"Oh, God," she said as she turned into the welcome arms of her new husband. Eleanor began to cry. The nurse came over to the gurney and gently closed Big Frank's eyes before she drew the sheet up over his face. Meg began to cry as well, her tears falling on the flower that Jeb wore in his lapel.

CHAPTER TEN

IT WAS a subdued pair who came back out of the tent from their interview. Dixon was paying strict attention to his car, walking slowly around its outside with a polishing cloth in his hand. Elmer Carter had found a booth with a jug of "cider" on a shelf underneath its counter, and was displaying a healthy rosy glow. The jug hadn't been difficult to find. In fact, the booth owner had offered him two more to take with him, and hadn't been refused. Gwen was outside the car, having just spotted Officer Stuart coming out of the hospital tent. The pair of them were practically nose to nose, recalling—whatever. And Baby Eleanor had gone back to sleep in Meg's arms.

Meg pulled Jeb to a stop before they came too close to the others. Passers-by she ignored. "What do you think, Jeb?"

"I think I love you. Let me hold the baby. Your arm must be about broken by now."

"No, not that." But she passed the child over to him anyway, and then rubbed her arm as if to restore circulation. "No. I mean what Frank said about Eleanor. He *gave* her to us. You can't give babies away like that!"

"It's hard to say," he said soberly. "Me not being a lawyer." He looked down at her, still dressed in the pristine white of her wedding gown. "But I know one thing—we can't hardly give the child back."

"Oh, you. This isn't a time for smart remarks."

172

"I know that," he returned as he put the child up on his shoulder. "There are lots of things you have to learn about me, Meg. One of them is that I have this sort of nervous condition. When something comes up in the conversation, and I have to stop and think about it, my lips keep flapping away, mostly with smart remarks that I don't even know are being said. It's a sort of defense mechanism that I can't control. I don't know what to think about Big Frank's gift. I know what he said. There aren't any more people left in his family. I know that Frank's dead. I know that Totie's dead. And I know we both want to keep the little girl, don't we?"

"Of course we do." Meg was following his conversation with deep concern. It was true that they were married, and yet what she knew about him—the inside "him"—could be written on the back of a postage stamp. And she wanted to know more. Wanted to know everything possible about Jeb Lacey. John Egemont Basil Lacey. It was hard not to giggle. It was an imposing name—but then he was an imposing man. "So what do we do?" she challenged him.

"We do something I mentioned to you some time ago," he said. "We have a problem in law—and I retain a smart old lawyer. We take our troubles to——"

"To Jesus," she interrupted. "He will carry you through. That's a real nice old hymn. One of my favorites."

"I'm sure it is, but I was thinking of a more mundane approach. We'll take our troubles to Harry Danvers."

"Your lawyer?"

"Our lawyer."

"Jeb," she said, "you are a wonderful man."

"Yes," he said modestly.

"And I'm going to kiss you."

"Why not? You deserve it. Even with this crowd around."

But wanting and doing were two separate things. After a preliminary try or two Meg found it almost impossible to kiss a man who was holding a nine-month-old baby on his shoulder. Not without squeezing the baby like a day-old loaf of bread.

"Gwen," she yelled. Twenty steps away her sister-in-law was still nose to nose with Sergeant Wendell Stuart of the police. "Gwen," she yelled again, at the top of her voice. No response.

But something was happening that Meg hadn't ever thought about. A small crowd was gathering around the tall beautiful girl in the wedding dress. An appreciative crowd, doing their best to hear every word. And now two or three of them, with help in mind, yelled, "Gwen!"

This was followed immediately by a mass yell from a dozen throats. "Gwen!" And this summons Gwen was unable to avoid. She stood tall for a moment and kissed the policeman on his cheek before she ambled over to Meg. "You called?"

"Yes. We have an emergency. Hold the baby." She snatched Eleanor away from Jeb and passed her to his sister. Startled, Gwen took possession without thinking.

"Now, John Egemont Basil..." Her arms went up around his neck, held on tightly, and she went up on tiptoes to seal off his mouth with her own. For a second he stood still, and then his own arms came around her, gently. There's something wrong here, Meg told herself. It was the sort of kiss she might get from Gran, and she didn't know what to do about it.

But he did.

There was a moment of waiting, as contact broke. "So," he whispered, "Meg Lacey doesn't know all there is to know about life."

She gave him an impish grin. "Life I know," she said. "I'm not all that sure about lust."

"You could easily learn," he said. "You have the aptitude." And before she could say another word his lips touched hers again. Touched and sealed. Fire ran up her backbone. Fire and joy and—love? There was a warming in the pit of her stomach such as she had never felt before. Her eyes closed, and she was immediately translated. They stood by a waterfall, and the music was punctuated with small claps of thunder. She was breathless—until he broke the seal.

"Like that," he said, with a very self-satisfied grin. Meg pulled herself back into the present, a dazed look on her face. It had started to rain again, and the little crowd around them were applauding. The re-routed parade had finally arrived, marching into the playground at full steam—still playing "Stars and Stripes Forever".

"Let's get out of here," her husband said.

"This baby's wet," Gwen said disgustedly. "And I don't mean from the rain."

"You keep fooling around with policemen and you're liable to find out more about wet babies than you want to know," her brother commented. His sister stuck her tongue out at him while Meg relieved her of her burden. The three of them dashed for the Cadillac and ducked inside.

Before the door slammed one of the men in the crowd came up to the car. "Don't run off now," he pleaded. "You two have a better act than the clowns, and that's for sure."

*   *   *

The big house on Virginia Street was packed to the rafters. People who ought to have known better were wandering around with drinks in hand telling off-color jokes and singing songs that even the army wouldn't allow. Dixon, who had left the car sitting in front of the porch, was moving around at high speed, trying to restore order. Some of the guests had been at the church; some of them were complete strangers who had wandered up from Windows restaurant after the oyster-shucking contest had ended.

"Friends of mine—watermen," Elmer Carter said. "Didn't seem reasonable to walk all the way out to the festival grounds in this rain. I brought some more of that cider that Big Frank was drinking. You don't mind?"

"Not a bit," Meg said. After all they were her husband's friends, and it wasn't the way for a wife to dispute them. Not on our first day of marriage together, anyway, she told herself, but you just wait, Jeb Lacey. I am for sure going to straighten you out some day soon.

She looked up at her husband. He was grinning like a fool, and hadn't had a single drink, as far as she knew. For just a minute one of those intimate little things that Gran had told her resounded through her mind. "You marry a man for what he is," the old lady had said, "not for what you would like to make him be!"

Meg shook her head and looked down at her empty hands. Empty? "My God, where's the baby?" she screamed. Jeb came hurtling out of the crowd. "I've lost Eleanor," she confessed to him.

"Nonsense. She's in her playpen," he said. "Put her there myself. Changed her diapers and put her there myself."

"Jeb Lacey, how could a man get drunk in five minutes?" she demanded. "Have I married a drinker?"

"Not me," he swore, raising his left hand and then quickly shifting to his right. "Unless you don't count the twenty minutes when we rode down from the festival grounds. Elmer had two jugs. Now he's only got one."

"If your mother could see you now," she said, sighing.

"Impossible. She's in Paris."

And the front doorbell rang. Dixon went to answer it. At that same moment the crowd in the study must have heard a real funny joke. Laughter lifted the ceiling. A woman screamed. Rex barked, and Eleanor began to cry. And a harsh feminine voice in the vicinity of the front door said, "Well, of course this is my house. My son's house. Same thing. Where has this crowd of reprobates come from? Where's the telephone? I'm going to call the police! And somebody tend to that stupid child! At once!"

Dixon, as big as he was, was backing away from the door. Slowly, but backing away nevertheless. A cone of silence seemed to project itself over the crowd, sucking up the noise like a massive blotter. Not a complete silence, but enough to make a noticeable difference.

Meg, despite her Old Methodist upbringing, had taken a drink to build up her courage. "Did you hear that?" she demanded of Jeb. " 'That stupid child!' That's what she said. I'm going to—— Who the devil can she be?"

Jeb, who had taken his full share of bottled goods, and because of his height could see over the heads of the crowd, took Meg's hand and held it tightly, saying, "I think you have the singular honor of meeting your mother-in-law." And he concluded with a small bow and a massive hiccup before he fell back into the chair Dixon managed to provide.

People began to eddy away from the front door, leaving a passage from the door directly to the living-room chair in which Jeb lolled. Meg gave him an angry shake, then stood up as tall as she could stretch. Mother-in-law was the magic word. She repeated them a time or two under her breath, and waited for lightning to strike.

The woman who stalked down that path was nothing like her son. She was barely five feet four in heels, her gray hair blued, half concealed by a perky little flowered hat, her rumpled silk suit an obvious Parisian style. She had a face that must once have been beautiful but now was scored with multiple lines and furrows. Her eyes were a faded blue; her figure was somewhat dumpy.

"I'm Mrs Nadine Lacey," she said in a gravelly voice. "Who are you and what have you done to my son?"

"Done to your son?" Meg took a deep breath and shook Jeb's shoulder again, to no avail. "I'll tell you. I'm Mrs Lacey too. Unfortunately I seem to have married your son. Twelve hours I've been Mrs Lacey. Have you been at it longer than that?"

Over the top of this lady's hat she could see Dixon ushering guests out the front door. The rain had stopped, and the crowd was thinning out rapidly. Elmer was the last to go. There was still a little something left in his jug. At least he took it away with him.

"Insolent little baggage," Nadine said, just as Eleanor began to yell for attention.

"Not little, by any means," Meg said. She headed for the study; the elder Mrs Lacey tried to race her, but lost. The baby was where she belonged, sitting up in her playpen. But Rex was sharing it with her, sitting proudly on guard, his massive muzzle over the top rail.

"A baby?"

"Well, yes," Meg said. "The hairy one is a dog." She bent over, snatched Eleanor up in her arms and cuddled her.

"So that's what you did," Nadine said. "Seduced him, and then claimed the baby was his! That's an old trick."

"Probably, but unfortunately the child is not Jeb's."

"Look, I understand problems like this," Jeb's mother said. "Single mothers have a difficult time. But my Jeb isn't the kind of man to pick on. Here." She opened her capacious purse and pulled out a small roll of bills. "Take this for yourself. There's five hundred dollars there. And then scoot out of here. A girl like you can find a man on any street corner."

"Maybe even a sober one," Meg commented. "But you know the lines—in sickness and in health, till death us do part. Alcoholism is a sickness for sure. And besides, I like the guy. In a funny sort of way he's an affectionate fellow. And when you get to my age there aren't many nice guys left, you know." While they were talking Meg wandered back to the living room, and Nadine followed her. Jeb was still sitting in his chair, grinning.

But there was something different about him. Something—he was concealing something, and not doing too well at it. In fact, Meg told herself, despite all the evidence, he's *not* drunk. He's trying to hide something—from me? He's being a ham actor, and—— "Till death us do part," she murmured. "Of course, I might kill him dead. Right now, for a fact!"

She turned back to Nadine. "And what do you think of your granddaughter, Mrs Lacey? Isn't she a darling? I'll bet you couldn't wait to become a grandmother."

"Dear God." The elder Mrs Lacey held up both hands to ward off fate. But fate could not be warded; Eleanor gurgled at her and reached out both hands. Meg, pushing the issue, handed the baby over to her grandmother. Eleanor reached for the fragile little hat and tore it off Nadine's head, throwing the string of curls at the side of her head into complete disarray.

"Oh, no!" Nadine Lacey rushed over to her son. "Jeb. Help me. The little monster attacked me, and this— woman—is hardly better."

Jeb shook his head and stood up gracefully. Meg snatched the baby out of Nadine's hands. "I'm not drunk, you know," he told them both. "I just wanted to see what kind of a person you had become, Mother. So you don't like my bride, you don't like my baby, and the only thing you do like is my money. Have I got that right?"

Meg, startled by all these Laceys, backed up and fell in Jeb's arms. "I thought you were——"

"Come now," Jeb interrupted, tongue-in-cheek. "I've spent the week talking to the Methodist minister. Don't smoke, don't drink, don't dance—I know a great deal about John Wesley's preaching."

He switched his aim. "So tell me, Mother, why did you come?"

"I—er—you invited me to your wedding," she replied weakly.

"Why, so I did!" he exclaimed. "How stupid can I get? It's nice of you to spend your money on such a long trip."

"I—ah—didn't exactly spend my own money, Jeb. I— er—charged it off on your credit card."

The smile vanished from Jeb's face. "Naughty, naughty," he said softly. "Would you believe that my lawyer and I have been talking about you?"

"Have you really?" A hopeful look.

"Yes. He and my accountant tell me that you spent eighty-five thousand of my hard-earned dollars this last year. Horses not running well?"

Meg cleared her throat. "If this is going to be a family discussion, I think I'll take Eleanor with me and go change my clothes. I'm still struggling with this wedding dress, and I'd like to get more comfortable."

"Yes. Go right ahead, love."

Meg headed for the stairs. Rex barked as she went by the study door. The big animal was still inside the playpen. He took three or four practise jumps, and finally let himself go. He soared. Perhaps that was the wrong word. He went up in the air, but his hind quarters failed to clear the top rail. When he came down his entire weight fell on that rail. The rail snapped, the playpen rolled up on its side, and Rex landed in the middle of his own sleeping rug.

"Nice work," Meg congratulated him. Rex circled around and settled on the rug as if that had been his destination all the while. And Eleanor cheered with enthusiasm.

A house full of quiet existed on the next floor. A feeble sun was doing its best to break through the windows. Outside the festival furor was dying down—regrettably dying down—as if the entire old city was already mourning its ending. "But they'll try it again next year, that's for sure," Meg told the baby. Eleanor gurgled in agreement.

Meg sat down on her bed and bounced the baby a time or two while she thought. He was *faking* all the time? Lord, I've got a lot to learn about this husband of mine. "But I do believe him," she assured Eleanor. "I do believe him. Eight years from now, when you claim your seat at the school, you'll see. We'll be together, happy as a pair of—clams? Or do I mean oysters?''

The downstairs door slammed. Dixon made soft noises to someone who had just come in. And then, loud and clear, came Gwen's voice. ''What are you doing here, Mother? I thought you would never give up your French living.'' A murmur from Mrs Lacey, and a reply from her daughter.

''Oh? Money?'' Meg heard a raucous laugh. ''Upstairs?''

Footsteps pounded on the stairs. She's running upstairs, Meg told herself. Why do I feel so old? I think I'd have to come up the stairs on hands and knees. It's been a long day, hasn't it, baby? Almost like forever. And now I'm a married lady and everything has to be different. Or does it? If I'm a fool to try to reform him, how much more so would he be if he tried to reform me? He knows all there is to know about John Wesley? Hah! All he knows is the outside of the package. But I'll—— No! What I'll do is be the best wife and mother I can be. Starting now. Eleanor needs her diapers changed!

And that was what she was doing when Gwen popped into the room.

Jeb's sister looked ten years younger than she had at the wedding. Dressed in trousers, a white blouse, and her hair well-combed, she was wearing the same sort of lopsided grin that made her brother so attractive.

''Meg, you'll never guess!'' Gwen pirouetted and leaned over to tickle the baby's bare stomach. ''Aren't babies cute?''

''Never guess what?'' And what has turned this vivacious creature from a baby-hater to this total admiration? she wondered. ''OK, I'll never guess. You'd better tell me.''

"Wendell and I——" The rest of it went clear over Meg's head. "Wendell and I"—of course, she thought. I can smell orange blossoms and wedding bells! The lines were fading from Gwen's forehead, as if some great authority had taken an iron and flattened them all out.

"And he understands why I—why I couldn't the first time, and he's been waiting all these years, and——" the baby kicked her heels under Meg's ministrations, and gurgled up a storm of chatter "—and we thought we'd just go over to the County Seat and ask Judge Partridge to do the honors, and——"

"And your mother's here and your brother's here and I'm here," Meg interrupted. "Why don't you just contact Reverend Stanton? I understand he's giving a special this month: two weddings for the price of one."

"Oh, you fool," Gwen gasped as she collapsed, laughing, on the bed. "That's only for young lovers and virgins, neither of which applies in my case. I wouldn't have the nerve to wear white. Here, let me help you with that dress."

Like most other things in her life, Meg's dress was a compromise. There were the traditional buttons down the back, but only for show. Hidden under the overlap of buttons was a most efficient zipper. Which had stuck when Meg had tried to do it for herself. Now, under Gwen's watchful eye and skilled fingers, it slid down and the dress collapsed.

"Not only could you wear white," Meg said, "but you could be a virgin. There's nothing in the ceremony that requires you to admit all your sins. All you need to vow is to love and honor, in sickness and in health——"

"Till death us do part," Gwen murmured. "I remember that part. And over at the festival you looked as if death was going to you part almost at once."

"Lookin' ain't doin'," Meg said. "He's still alive, isn't he? And I'd love to be a matron of honor. Or maybe my gran would do that. She seems to think right about now that all the Laceys are saints on earth."

There was no doubt that Gwen was Jeb's sister. She winked an eye at her sister-in-law. "And of course we are," she said, and laughed again.

So when Jeb came in a few minutes later, followed by Rex, questing at his heels, all three of the females were laughing their fool heads off.

"Something's funny?" he asked.

"You wouldn't believe. Where's Mother?"

"I sent her over to the Urbanna Inn for the night, while she thinks about the offer I made her."

"Offer? Why does that make me suspicious?" Meg asked. But with Eleanor kicking up her heels in her crib, and Gwen rolling over on the bed, still laughing, there seemed to be little else for Meg to do. She came around the end of the crib, stretched herself up on the tips of her toes, threw her arms around his neck, and turned him with a kiss that rocked him back on his heels.

"Great gobs of golden goose grease," he murmured as he struggled for breath. "Where did you learn to do that?"

"I had a wonderful teacher," she said demurely. "The Duke of Moldavia."

"C'mon now," Gwen protested. "None of that stuff in front of us two virgins. What did you do to my mother?"

Jeb stared at his sister. "I have this problem with my hearing," he said. "I think tomorrow I'll—no, the day after tomorrow I'll go uptown and get my ears checked. I told *your* mother that I was going to put her on a spendthrift trust."

"So all right, I confess," his sister said. "What's that?"

"I'm going to establish a fund for her, from which she can only withdraw the interest. And she'll have to live on that interest without any further help from me."

"Good lord, and you expect her to live in Paris like that? She'll find a way to wiggle out of the restrictions in no time."

"I don't think so," Jeb said. "First of all, she's finished with Paris. We still own Grandfather's house in Memphis and that's where she's going to live—or lose all the money. And the trust is going to be administered by our lawyer, Harry Danvers."

"Well, she won't be able to get any help from us," Gwen said. "Wendell and I are going to live on a policeman's salary until he finishes college. Did I tell you that he's enrolled in the Virginia Commonwealth Law School? The classes are all at night, and he's going to be a lawyer, and—well, by that time you'll need another lawyer, brother. And you'll hire Wendell at a fabulous salary, which will be a lot less than what I've been chiseling off you for the past seven years!"

Jeb scratched his head and gave Meg a one-handed hug. "I'm darned if it doesn't make a sort of sense," he said. "And by the way, wife, next Monday Harry has arranged for us to appear in court on the adoption of Eleanor Frances."

Meg Lacey had trouble with a tear that kept trying to run down her cheek. "Y-you..." she stuttered. "You've managed to clear up every problem in our family. You're a wonderful man, Jeb Lacey." And there was such a worshipful look on her face that her sister-in-law suppressed her giggles.

"Yes, I suspect you're right," Jeb said.

"I'm going over to see Wendell," Gwen said. "He has to explain all this to his mother and father. And I believe I'll take this kid along with me. It's so much easier explaining things to a prospective mother-in-law when you have a cute little baby along."

But the other adult pair were so busy with their own thoughts and needs that they hardly paid attention—it seemed. I've got him trapped, Meg told herself as she felt the warmth of him against her taffeta slip and recognized the countless urges that were running up and down her spine. It all seemed so real—until he broke the kiss and yelled after his sister, "And you could take the dog as well!"

The boat was old and tired and comfortable, loaned to them by Elmer Carter, Jeb's buddy from war days. It was anchored in the quiet waters of Urbanna Creek, just under the hill where Rosegil House was located. Across the water they could see lights gleaming in the old customs house, where Gwen Lacey and her significant other, Wendell Stuart, were spending the night as overseers of Eleanor Frances Lacey.

The festival had ended officially at ten in the evening, and now, just after one in the morning, the streets were empty of people and only trash blew across the center of town. The skies had cleared. A three-quarter moon was examining what was usually the cleanest town in Virginia. But tomorrow would see to that. Tomorrow and tomorrow, until it was November again, and time for another Oyster Festival.

Meg leaned back on the over-sized bunk and grinned at her husband. He was nursing a big coffee mug and gnawing on a tuna-fish sandwich. "So how did you convince your sister to baby-sit for us?"

"Hey, that was the easy part," he said between chews. "She and Wendell—that's a tough family to break into. They're all Baptists, you know. When I offered her an empty house she jumped at the chance."

"You know she's decided to get married in the same church we used? I'm a little worried about that."

"Worried?"

"Well, she's not a——"

"And neither were we," he said, chuckling. "But it didn't seem to matter."

"No. I suppose not. But it's all so—you know, I never could understand girls who—did that—before marriage. I never realized what a wonderful—exercise it is." She brushed her long gold hair back and patted the bed beside her. "And now what are we going to do?"

"Sleep?" he suggested.

"Oh? You mean that's—we're—you're——?"

"That's exactly what I mean." He walked across the cabin just as the wake of a passing power boat hit them and threw him on top of her. Before he could restore his balance she hugged him closer. The shoestring strap of her nightgown had slipped off her shoulder, leaving her breast quivering an inch or two from his lips. She could feel his unexpected arousal.

"Oh, hell," he muttered as his lips closed on her hardened nipple.

"As you say, husband," she murmured. "Just a few more oysters and you'll be——"

"Shut up and lie down," he commanded. "You and I have some talking to do."

"Yes, of course. Talking," Margarete Lacey said. "If you think you're able...?"

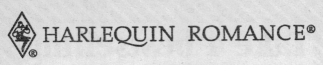

HARLEQUIN ROMANCE®

Coming Next Month

#3379 BRIDES FOR BROTHERS Debbie Macomber
The first book in Midnight Sons, a very special new six-book series from this bestselling author.

Welcome to Hard Luck, Alaska. Location: 50 miles north of the Arctic Circle. Population: 150—but it'll be growing soon! Because this town is determined to attract women. The campaign is spearheaded by the O'Halloran brothers, who run a small-plane charter service called Midnight Sons. Thanks to them, things are going to change in Hard Luck—maybe more than anyone expects....

In *Brides for Brothers* meet Sawyer O'Halloran, one of the Midnight Sons, and Abbey Sutherland from Seattle, librarian and divorced mother of two young children. Abbey's the first of the women to arrive in Hard Luck—but she hasn't told anyone she's arriving with kids!

#3380 THE BEST MAN Shannon Waverly
Kayla Brayton remembered Matt Reed as a handsome, self-assured twenty-one-year-old, and she fully expected a handsome, self-assured thirty-one-year-old. She wasn't disappointed! Matt was the kind of man every girl dreamed of, but was he the best man for her?

#3381 ONCE BURNED Margaret Way
Family Ties
Guy Harcourt was strong, forceful and dynamic. He was also irresistible to women. And Celine Langston was no exception. She had never wanted anyone as much as him. But she was like a moth caught in a candle's flame, and once burned...

#3382 LEGALLY BINDING Jessica Hart
Sealed with a Kiss
Jane was a sensible girl—everyone said so. Ten years ago she'd been far too sensible to run away with the local rebel, Lyall Harding. But now Lyall was back and the bad boy had grown into a successful businessman. Was now the time to throw caution to the wind?

AVAILABLE THIS MONTH:

As a Privileged Woman,
you'll be entitled to all these Free Benefits.
And Free Gifts, too.

To thank you for buying our books, we've designed an exclusive FREE program called *PAGES & PRIVILEGES™*. You can enroll with just one Proof of Purchase, and get the kind of luxuries that, until now, you could only read about.

BIG HOTEL DISCOUNTS

A privileged woman stays in the finest hotels. And so can you—at up to 60% off! Imagine standing in a hotel check-in line and watching as the guest in front of you pays $150 for the same room that's only costing you $60. Your *Pages & Privileges* discounts are good at Sheraton, Marriott, Best Western, Hyatt and thousands of other fine hotels all over the U.S., Canada and Europe.

FREE DISCOUNT TRAVEL SERVICE

A privileged woman is always jetting to romantic places. When you fly, just make one phone call for the lowest published airfare at time of booking—or double the difference back! PLUS—you'll get a $25 voucher to use the first time you book a flight AND 5% cash back on every ticket you buy thereafter through the travel service!

HR-PP5A

FREE GIFTS!

A privileged woman is always getting wonderful gifts. Luxuriate in rich fragrances that will stir your senses (and his). This gift-boxed assortment of fine perfumes includes three popular scents, each in a beautiful designer botle. <u>Truly Lace</u>...This luxurious fragrance unveils your sensuous side. L'Effleur...discover the romance of the Victorian era with this soft floral. <u>Muguet des bois</u>...a single note floral of singular beauty.

FREE INSIDER TIPS LETTER

A privileged woman is always informed. And you'll be, too, with our free letter full of fascinating information and sneak previews of upcoming books.

MORE GREAT GIFTS & BENEFITS TO COME

A privileged woman always has a lot to look forward to. And so will you. You get all these wonderful FREE gifts and benefits now with only one purchase...and there are no additional purchases required. However, each additional retail purchase of Harlequin and Silhouette books brings you a step closer to even more great FREE benefits like half-price movie tickets... and even more FREE gifts.

L'Effleur...This basketful of romance lets you discover L'Effleur from head to toe, heart to home.

Truly Lace... A basket spun with the sensuous luxuries of Truly Lace, including Dusting Powder in a reusable satin and lace covered box.

Complete the Enrollment Form in the front of this book and mail it with this Proof of Purchase.

PROOF OF PURCHASE
Offer expires October 31, 1996

HR-PP5